And Now....

First Edition published 2025 by

2QT Limited (Publishing)

United Kingdom

Printed in Great Britain by IngramSpark

A CIP catalogue record for this book is available
from the British Library

ISBN 978-1-0684439-0-9

And Now...

FRANK ENGLISH

"I can't believe she's gone," Ross Senior muttered as he gazed almost absent-mindedly at his daughter, Rosie, across their busy breakfast table as light from the early morning Mediterranean sunshine ricocheted across the old mahogany table's silver and crystal setting blindingly, forcing Rosie to replace her sunglasses quickly.

"We—" he went on repetitively sadly.

"Enjoyed your life together enormously, I think," she interrupted, hoping to deflect and absorb the abject sadness that had all-but consumed him.

"I suppose," he returned quietly after a moment or two of silent thought.

"She wouldn't have wanted you to stop … living," his daughter tried to reassure him, realising that she might have an uphill struggle as he felt there was no joy or purpose left in his life.

"There often doesn't feel there's any point in going on," he murmured, barely able to be heard. "After all, *I* was supposed to have been the one to go first, and—"

"Not the way how it works, Father," she interrupted, feeling more than a little frustrated after five months of grieving.

"You are supposed to grieve but also to get on with your life. What would Nell have said had the roles been reversed? And *that's* a rhetorical question because we both know the answer. Don't we?"

Her last words were not meant as a placatory soft uttering, trying to cajole a person feeling sorry for itself. She had come across quite a lot of Aussie philosophy while dealing with other people's emotions before she hit England's 'soft touch' approach. *That* way of dealing with self-centred self-pity didn't sit well with her, especially after such a lengthy period of introversion in the land of her birth. He had to snap out of it!

"I'd like your help today, Father," Rosie interjected sharply after she had cleared the breakfast pots, and he had shuffled over to his favourite chair on the veranda overlooking the ocean. "Father?"

"Heard you, my dear," he replied with a half-smile. "Just trying to decide what it might be that you need. It can't be money because you have enough of your own. So, it must be…"

"Advice, and your knowledge of the property market hereabouts," she interrupted gently. "We discussed my acquiring an appropriate property close by a while ago. Remember?"

"Indeed, I do," he assured her. "I've not forgotten, you realise. In fact, there is an apartment in a similar block to this one just fifty yards away."

"Sounds interesting…" she returned eagerly, shuffling her chair up to his. "Tell me more."

"He's not here anymore, Mother," Toby insisted again. "I know it's hard. I miss him as well as you, but we can't become stuck in the past. He might not have been the best companion in the early days, but you have to remember what he did for us latterly. He dragged us out of the gutter and gave us a future that we have to develop."

"What do you mean 'develop'?" she asked, a worried and sad look growing.

"Thereby hangs a problem," her son began to explain. "We may have enough money to live a reasonable life on what he has given us, but I for one am not prepared to sit at home and stagnate. Your husband and my stepfather wouldn't have wanted us not to do … stuff. I'm sure he would have wanted us to get on and become active."

"I'm not sure," Jenny replied, lips pursed tightly. "We – he and I – were about to live the quiet but comfortable life we had never experienced. We expected no more, but, if you remember, he wanted *you* to succeed, and to that end he left you this envelope, I think."

She handed him an ornate envelope scrawled with Jonas's inimitable signature and ornately sealed in wax.

"What's this?" Toby queried, not expecting any more than he had already received from him.

"I have no idea," his mother muttered quietly. "Perhaps you had better open it to find out."

"It's a letter of introduction to a chap in Richmond that is hoping to set up a taxi service in the area," he explained after a few moments of quiet reading. "Apparently our Lanchester motor car will be very much in demand as a taxi for rich people, from which we will be able to earn a very good living."

"Taxi?" she puzzled. "What's that?"

"It's a means of providing transport for people that may want to travel privately and quietly from one place to another," Toby explained. "Well now, that's a turn up. Fancy him thinking of something like that."

"What will happen to the motor?" Jenny asked not sure really what he was talking about. "Will it still be yours?"

"Certainly will!" he uttered once he had finished reading. "It seems like I will only need to pay a small amount to the person setting up the company for any business he puts my way. A no-lose venture, I think, that I will have to look into."

He occupied his stepfather's once favourite chair, a satisfied air about him. This was what he was talking about. Freedom to pursue a paid job he might enjoy doing while making money of his own.

"We could end up being really … rich," Toby sniggered. "Who'd have thought it, eh?"

"So, we won't have to move from here, then?" his mother asked, not too sure what he was talking about really.

"No, but we have to get one of those new-fangled contraptions called a 'telephone'," he went on, a look of excitement growing.

"What's one of those and … why?" Jenny asked, again no idea what he was talking about.

"A machine you hold to your ear and mouth so you can talk to people who live elsewhere," he explained. "Apparently, you can speak to other people in many other countries now without having to be near them. And, before you ask, mother dear, it's all done by … magic!"

He giggled internally, seeing the look of shock and horror on her face.

～

"I think I like that one," Rosie muttered as she wandered in her mind from bare hallway to the gloriously large living room, with that wonderful view of the Mediterranean from the front balcony. "There perhaps needs to be one or two alterations to be made, but basically, hopefully it will fulfil all my needs."

"It's very similar to the condition Nell and I encountered with ours when we first took it over," her father said quietly, a palpable look of reminiscence overtaking him. He fell silent as his Australian daughter wandered around.

"Perhaps a new bathroom needed?" she observed. "What do you say, Father?"

"Shower and a new Crapper I should think," he agreed. "For me, having spent a large stretch in your neck of the woods, a shower is the only way, with a new streamlined flushing lavatory."

"I like the fact also that it has an elevator to save struggling up four flights of steps," Rosie added. "Can't top that it's a penthouse, and this balcony gives me just what I need, particularly first thing in the morning."

"Otis," her father slipped into the conversation.

"I beg your pardon, Father?" she muttered, a profoundly puzzled look settling in her face.

"The Otis is what allowed us to access this top floor of the apartment block," he tried to explain. "An *elevator* that in England is otherwise known as a *lift*. Invented in 1852 by Elisha Otis in Yonkers, New York."

They both laughed at his deliberate attempted American pronunciation as she linked his arm and drew his unresisting body closer to her. Having spent the last five years searching for a father to call her own, she still couldn't believe how luck seemed to have dropped him in her lap. Although Nell hadn't been her mother, she still felt a profound sadness that they had lost her in such upsetting circumstances.

An unexpected silence had engulfed them as they watched and listened to the spitting and roaring motor car engines during their brief journey back along the dazzling Promenade des Anglais so close to the captivating blue of the Mediterranean Ocean.

"I think I have found my forever home, Father," Rosie said quietly without allowing her gaze to be drawn away from such a spectacular view.

Snuggling closer to his daughter on his veranda, Ross said, "If you are sure, we had better complete the deal so that no-one else might steal it from you. You have no idea how happy this makes me, although you could still stay with me if you wanted to."

"I will always be close by whenever you need me," she said softly, holding his unprotesting body close to hers. "You will never know how long I have yearned for moments like this."

"Hello!" a lilting female voice wafted over them. "Anybody home?"

Rosie stiffened and turned to her father, a puzzled frown descending from her brow.

"Somebody I'd like you to meet," he said as he prised himself slowly from the balcony's comfortably easy settee he loved so much nowadays.

"In here!" he shouted, this encounter enlightening his face. He loved his new-found daughter dearly, but here was someone to delight his soul while sharing his remaining years.

"Grandpa Ross!" a beautiful young lady threw herself into his waiting arms, as their tears mixed within their embrace. "I am so sorry…"

"No need, my beautiful – and famous – young lady," he added quietly, as his daughter joined them.

"Rosie," he started, "I should like you to meet my grand-daughter, Poppy Spence. You have a lot in common that I am sure you will share. Poppy, this is my … daughter, Rosie."

"Daughter? … Granddaughter?" the two young ladies gasped in harmony, neither knowing what to make of this unexpected announcement.

Chapter 2

"Does it really matter?" Annabel asked quite simply.

"Of course it does!" George insisted forcibly. "It always matters."

"Your parents didn't think so," she replied with a persuasive smile. "Has it ever made any difference to *your* life? Or to that of your sisters, for that matter?"

"And by that you mean?" George replied sharply.

"Well … the fact that you were born … out of wedlock?" she responded carefully slowly.

George was stunned into alarmed silence, not knowing how to respond to what seemed like a thoughtless jibe.

A brooding silence grew, engulfing them both, until a feeling of animosity overcame George, making him feel less in control than he liked. Why were they having this conversation when all he wanted … hoped … to do was to wait until they were man and wife before consummating their love for each other. Not too much to ask when they were only a matter of two weeks away, he felt.

He hadn't known about his parents never finding the time to wed until it was too late – a situation that his sisters shared with degrees of animosity that, with time, had grown into acceptance. After all, how could that illegitimacy affect their life now?

His old adversary, anger, began to well up inside, persuading him to lift his tired body and to leave the room, unsure of where this seemingly unnecessary confrontation was about to lead him. He had followed this line with the love of his life, Poppy, before, allowing his negativity to stoke the animosity they had shared towards the end of *their* relationship.

Although he knew he should never have allowed his temper to lead him down this destructive path, it was inevitably entrenched in his psyche that he couldn't – or didn't want to – change.

"George! Don't go … please!" she pleaded as she heard the outside door click shut, realising that she had hit a sore point and that *that* was, perhaps, not the way to cement their sexual relationship. She desperately had to find a plausible way to keep her secret that must not – at any cost – leave the safety of her own mind.

The stable was quiet, and a place that offered him silence and solace from all the irritating and confrontational issues he had to face on a daily basis. No matter how often he promised himself he wouldn't react, a tiny switch in his mind always broke that urge, allowing his anger to spring out of control. Silence away from the irksome presence of non-understanding humans was the only way his anger could be brought back under control – until the next time. Poppy was the only person that could come close to keeping him on an even keel.

Why did Annabel insist, knowing about his views on sex out of marriage? Was there something – some secret – underlying it all? How—?

"George?" a familiar soft voice sought him from the stable door, creaking as it moved in the late evening breeze. "You in there?"

"Florence?" his surprised and startled voice replied. "How did you know I'd be in here?"

"Sister's intuition," she responded as she approached. "Problems with Annabel?"

"Don't hold back will you Sister dear?" he replied, knowing that she never cut corners and always said it as she saw it. After all, she was Yorkshire. "I can always trust you to be honest and … blunt, can't I?"

"Is there any other way?" she guffawed. "Well? Problems?"

"Can't hide from you, can I, Gypsy Rose Lee?" he answered, a wan smile twitching his lips.

Wandering slowly in what used to be the dairy, he explained where they stood, a concerned look gathering on his sister's face throughout his explanation.

"Is there something you're not telling me?" he urged, seeing the state of her face. "Come on now! Out with it!"

Beckoning him to sit down on a hay bale, she started her explanation which left George quiet and speechless.

"And how do you know this?" he asked quietly, stunned by what he had heard.

"It's common knowledge," she replied with a dismissive shrug.

"Common knowledge?" he questioned quickly. "Then how is it that I didn't know?"

"You're a man. That's why," she muttered sharply. "You live and work in a man's world not knowing anything about a woman's place in it. You are so different from the vast majority of your fellow creatures who—"

"How different?" he butted in sharply.

"Honestly?" she added, daring him to want to pursue her narrative.

"What else?" he said, taken aback somewhat by her pointed response. "Haven't I always been truthful as long as you've known me?"

"I have to give you that," she agreed. "But are you honest with yourself and your belief in what you are accepting from someone that has walked away from you at least once already?"

"I—" he hesitated, confused by what she was saying.

"Her stuff about loss of her job and accommodation was partly right," his sister went on. "What she told you about her circumstance was lacking in some very important details."

"How do you mean?" he questioned, not understanding what she was trying to tell him. "Spit it out woman!"

Florence's explanation was quietly delivered, obliging her brother to sit and listen without interruption but not without a surprised, a shocked and painful look gathering in his eyes. *That* he never expected in a million years.

"Where did you get all this … information from?" he asked. Not too sure whether to believe it all. "Are you sure of your facts?"

"I am, but why don't you try asking her?" his sister suggested. "She's just coming in … and I'm just going out."

Florence nodded quietly at Annabel as they passed in the doorway, without exchanging any greetings.

Although a sombre mood had invaded Boulders Wood following the unexpected and untimely death of its former mistress in a foreign land several months before, her memory and presence remained. Time since the event had passed slowly when much had to be said about her legacy. No-one was more affected than Mary with whom she had worked unstintingly as a sister-in-arms for more than forty years.

For those responsible for the daily survival of the farm, life had to go on without reprieve.

Ross had extra responsibilities heaped upon his more than ample shoulders as not only did he have his daily farm duties to see to, his wife, Martha, was having problems with her pregnancy. This was now in its last, uncomfortable and unwelcome four weeks and she couldn't wait to reach its end. How she would dearly love to return to the times before its onset when she would be able to spend time with her loving daughter and her uncomplaining and very attentive husband. Had it not been for his support, she would have thrown in the towel long before.

"This one is pushing me to the edge, Ross," she had warned him on more than one occasion. "I so wish with all my heart it was over."

"It will be soon, my sweet lady," he soothed, his arms clasping the love of his life to his body as he helped her from her crib.

She winced with a sharp intake of breath when her feet touched the flock rug next to her side of the bed which took the edge from the cold oak flooring. That had been one of the first things Ross had done to improve the comfort of their bedroom – oak floorboarding was so much more comfortable than its predecessor.

"Ross!" Martha gasped as she grasped the bedroom door frame on her way to the indoor toilet that had been installed a short time before. "I think it's on the move. I need Dr Twist. Please!"

"I can see the distinct resemblance," Poppy uttered quietly but with more than a little frisson of excitement after Ross's explanation.

"And so can I," Ross added as he wheeled in a shiny trolly bearing tea and cakes to share. "You could even be sisters from what I can see."

"Or even … aunt and niece?" Poppy observed. "For technically that's what we are. Welcome to the family, Rosie."

"And yet, we are not many years apart," Rosie added with a giggle.

"But which one is older?" Poppy replied, a knowing smile spreading.

"Thereby hangs a tale," Ross retorted. "One I can only guess at because I was present at neither event, unfortunately, and could only enjoy the pleasure years later. Each experience will stay with me for the rest of the time I am on this earth – for however long that may be."

A heavy silence engulfed the trio, drawing in a darkness that none expected or felt comfortable within. Suddenly the golden rays of a magnificent sun burst through the balcony's frosted inner doors lightening the lounge in which they were sitting, allowing them to glorify in the warmth they had come to enjoy on a regular basis.

"Unbelievable!" was all the two girls could mouth as the uncompromising view of the Mediterranean Sea grabbed at their eyes once they had been drawn on to the balcony again.

The Promenade des Anglais was crowded with holidaying bodies that intermingled with rich and not-so-rich alike, jostling for space to adjust to the sun's warmth, and to soak up the electrifying atmosphere. The advent of four-wheeled vehicles had enhanced *and* violated the restful ethos of pre-twentieth century holidaying in such an exciting venue in a way that a return to those heady times was certain never to happen.

⌒〜

"Have you ever thought of this new-fangled 'telephone' service that has been invented recently?" Dr Twist asked, mildly sarcastically. "It's very useful you know."

"I've heard of it," Ross answered more than a little urgency decorating his response. "Neither time nor expense will allow its introduction here at Boulders Wood, I fear Doc."

"Anyway," the medic said, rolling down his shirt sleeves and beginning to replace his jacket, "you might like to reconsider your decision in light of incidents like this one. Your wife will need hospital help to deliver your new child as safely as possible. I alerted an ambulance before I came, and as I can detect horses' hooves, she will be away within moments."

A hefty banging at the front door corroborated the doctor's words as the twin oaken doors burst open and two medical orderlies dressed in white, hurried into the room as Dr Twist had directed. Clattering up the stark wooden stair well they were ushered into the bedroom where Martha lay in excruciating pain.

"I believe the baby has its umbilical cord wrapped reasonably tightly round its neck," Dr Twist added urgently. "Touch and go I'm afraid, unless your wife and soon-to-be child are able to receive the attention they so urgently require. You can accompany them in the ambulance if you wish."

The orderlies descended the stairs with Martha, providing just about enough support from their makeshift stretcher, and out to the horse-drawn ambulance. It stopped outside Joseph and Lilly Victoria's cottage to pick up Ross who had hot-footed it to alert them of the situation before it gathered speed at a leisurely trot to Mount Pleasant Emergency Maternity Home.

C H A P T E R   3

"Do we need to become enemies over something that we can surely sort out between us?" Annabel ventured quickly as she sat next to her man, sliding her hand onto his ample thigh.

He turned towards her slowly, a hard look growing in his face as he removed her hand firmly. "What's his name, Annabel?"

"I don't … understand," she replied slowly after a moment's hesitation, a dithering frown betraying her growing apprehension.

"The man that threw you out on the street," he continued. "The man that didn't want you to bear the child you are carrying. You know … the reason you wanted to have sex before it became obvious that you are already … pregnant?"

"I don't know what to … say," she muttered quietly. "What makes you think I am with child?"

"I *know* you are!" he insisted, a sharp ire rising. "Wanting me to believe that this impending child would be the product of our 'physical' relationship that has no existence yet."

"I—" she blustered, concerned that she had been found out.

"No, you are not!" he growled aggressively. "And … you need to pack your stuff and get off back to your parents' place because I know you lied about them as well. You've got an hour to clear out."

He jumped to his feet quickly and, aiming his boot at a non-existent object in his path, he stormed out of the stable to ready himself for his late morning local deliveries.

Annabel sat back on a huge hay bale cursing herself for her lack of honesty and trust in George's good nature. Now here he was, an unforgiving enemy for life, unable to forgive her for the second time she had tried to persuade him she could be trusted.

Panic began to set in as she started to realise that any attempt at trying to persuade George to relent would be doomed to failure. He was intransigent in the extreme when his anger took charge because of some deliberate misdeed, and that intransigence would only worsen.

~

'Had this really been a good idea?' George thought as he looked at his small flock of Swaledale sheep before he ventured out to check on his Herdwicks. He *knew* they would be fine, but he felt that he owed it to them to make sure.

Although he considered his decision had been final when he had undertaken the plan to replace all his bovine stock with these woolly creatures, he had been beset at times with his usual doubts on the new adventure. Prior to selling on his herd and going it alone with the sheep in discussion with Ross and Joseph, he had been persuaded to consider returning to their original partnership to enhance the success of both Boulders Wood and Garside Farms. This would begin to build strong foundations with cattle and sheep, ensuring that they would be able to support one another through growth and stagnation.

Still, as per George's sometimes unstable personality, he had allowed doubts to creep into most decisions he had made. The one concerning Annabel was no different. Did he really want her to go, leaving him in depression once again, struggling to sustain his occasional positive take on life?

"I'm sorry, George," a quietly apologetic voice crept over his shoulder, causing him to start. "I know I should have told you about my condition, but I did really want to be with you. My big mistake was to leave you the last time we were together. I can understand why I would have wanted it to work out between us because you—"

He spun round quickly to see Annabel and her baggage seemingly ready to leave.

"Please stay, Annabel," he said urgently quietly. "I tend to make rash decisions which later I regret, and if you leave, I won't forgive myself for its result."

Annabel threw her arms about his neck as tears started to stream down her cheeks. They kissed unapologetically passionately, as her handbag dropped from her hand, and held each other closely not wishing to let go.

"Time to unpack and start as we mean to go on, eh?" George urged taking her hand in one of his and lifting her one small luggage bag as they turned to regain their home. Linking his arm, head resting on his muscular shoulder, they regained the house and headed for the bedroom.

⁓

A gentle tap on the front door of Boulders Wood caught Ross's attention as he finished mashing a pot of tea. He had not been long home from the maternity hospital having been advised by the medical staff that there was nothing he could do there as his wife was under necessary sedation.

"Hello. Good morning, Rosie," he greeted the young lady cheerfully. "I thought you were in the South of France enjoying its glorious sunshine, with an occasional dip in the Mediterranean?"

"I beg your pardon!" she uttered, taken aback by this hunk of a man she had never seen before.

"It *is* Rosie, isn't it?" he asked, immediately unsure of whom he thought this lady might be. "You were here not that long ago, seeking a certain 'Ross Booth'. Weren't you?"

"I have no idea what you are talking about," she uttered, a very puzzled shake of the head heralding her ignorance. "I *am* looking for my father who happens to be called Ross … Booth, and whom I have been told lives here. Are you him? My name is Sarah … Sarah Booth."

"Please come in Miss … Booth," Ross invited her. "Tea is in the pot mashing. May I offer you something to eat?"

At that moment an upstairs bedroom door bounced open and his daughter, Annie, careered down the stairs, to be followed closely by Joseph's daughters, Jessie and Joanie, and their mother Lilly Victoria.

Annie threw herself at her father who caught her and threw her in the air accompanied by her squeals of joy.

"How are things at the hospital, Ross?" Lilly Victoria asked, careful not to convey her feelings of disquiet concerning her sister, Martha.

"Progress, I feel," he replied, quickly changing the subject. "This young lady is—"

"We know!" the three girls squealed with delight as they threw their arms around the newcomer.

"She's Rosie, your sister," Annie went on a puzzled look developing. "Silly Daddy."

"Sister?" Sarah puzzled. "But I don't *have* a brother ... or a sister."

"The 'Rosie' we are talking about is the daughter of my father, Ross, and his neighbour in Australia. She was called Betty," Ross explained.

"Betty?" Sarah ventured. "She was my mother's sister...?"

The room fell silent with shocked surprise, as Ross and Lilly Victoria exchanged puzzled glances.

"I think you will find that your real mother, Betty, is also that of your twin sister, Rosie, too," Ross continued. "Your sister experienced the same feelings as well when she found out the truth."

"That would make you Rosie's twin sister," Lilly Victoria suggested. "And her identical twin, by the looks of it."

Sarah sat down on the settee with an unexpected bump, the kitchen door opening as Mary-Jane backed into the room, a tray of buttered and jammed scones, slices of Victoria sponge, and sandwiches on a large wooden tray. Setting this on the table, she retreated to bring another tray bearing an enormous, steaming brown tea pot and umpteen pieces of relevant crockery and cutlery.

Sarah's face simply stared in shock at the enormity of such a spread as she had never seen before. Could she have stepped into her heaven on earth, as Mary-Jane set to cutting and dividing and plating such a fabulous feast.

<hr>

"Goodness!" Annabel gasped, with her eyes closed as she drew the bed clothes to cover her naked body. "I've never—"

"We are going to be married soon officially, aren't we?" George drew her unprotesting but quivering body to his. "I have begun to feel that that isn't as important as I had considered it to be, and, although *we* know differently, the child you are carrying will be mine."

"You have no idea how good that feels for me, George," she responded as she drew him onto her again.

Florence and Charity's voices mingled downstairs as the front door clicked shut.

"How is your writing getting on?" Charity asked her sister to the clatter of crockery in the kitchen not twenty feet below the bedroom that George and Annabel now occupied, obliging them to dress and confront sisters that had no ideas about their now growing relationship. As far as they were concerned, their brother's business was his own as long as he was aware about what he was letting himself in for. Charity had her own life with her man and their nippers. Florence had discovered the joy of writing stories from which others perhaps might derive enjoyment and satisfaction. She had watched how it had driven Poppy McIntyre to begin to achieve *her* goals which had not only encouraged Florence to pursue that aim but had set her on a course to emulate *her* successes.

Poppy had always offered to help should Florence feel the need, but she had always felt the need to tread her own path, even if that path mirrored Poppy's to some extent.

"George!" Florence called as he entered the room quietly, with a vague look of surprise flicking across her face. "You startled me. I thought you would have been in the fields with your woolly friends. Annabel?"

"Preparing to cook tea eventually, I believe," he responded a little hesitantly.

"Is she … all right?" his sister asked tentatively.

"She's fine," he responded firmly. "We have been planning our wedding that needs to be organised very soon. Time's moving on and we're not getting any younger."

C H A P T E R 4

Saturday morning. Almost five to nine. Centre of Richmond in Yorkshire's North Riding. Early May, with a good-humoured queue beginning to form outside Mary's Pantry, drawn to that food emporium by the gloriously mouth-watering odours of baking goodies that were escaping through the shop's tiny front line open windows. This was a daily occurrence that had brought – nose first – so many lovers of exquisite food to this place for several years.

Luckily for them another, similar, but tantalisingly different pâtisserie, had opened next door very recently and was putting out scents to titillate deeper palate tastes.

Mary-Jane's kitchen has arrived with the proverbial BANG! Open only two days, her clientele was now metaphorically drooling over the tastes and aromas that were very different from those produced by its next-door older sister.

Concerns had been expressed by Mary's husband, Geoffrey, as to the wisdom of opening another 'competitor' just feet away from the original shop. His concerns evaporated very quickly once the new emporium opened its wares to the discerning population. Not only had his concern about the perceived lack of success been wiped unceremoniously away, but the original exquisite outlet had become more successful too.

Customers found it hard to believe that two similar, but very different outlets could not only succeed, but each support the other, drawing in even more customers hungry for what they had to offer.

"All right. All right," Geoffrey conceded. "I was wrong. But—"

"All you had to do was trust in my judgement," Mary butted in with an enormous grin decorating her face, supported by her niece's quietly happy giggle. To have become so popular after only two days was unheard of in the very early part of the twentieth century when poverty had become rife.

Mary, in her way, had heightened the quandary and had contributed to feeding some of the unfortunate and unlucky down-and-outs in her area.

Ginny Brown and her family – Maisie and Jimmy – had been a prize example. They had never experienced a 'normal' life until Mary and Geoffrey had appeared on the scene, and Ross had dispatched her bullying thug of a partner unceremoniously. The cottage they now inhabited at a short distance from the dairy that Ross had taken from Garside Farm and set up in a barn behind Boulders Wood to allow Annabel, Ginny and Charity to work, had also been refurbished and added to.

Ross was pleased he had reinstated and refurbished the dairy in a much more convenient place, both for access for the staff and the size of the building. Although they had tentatively set up a loose association between the two farms – Boulders Wood and Garside – nothing official had yet been agreed. The two businesses had grown further apart, leaving George Garside to go it alone and to organise his own business affairs.

Initially the Garside Farm seemed to be stuttering somewhat – as new businesses often do – but the more involved George became with his sheep, the more stable and forward-looking it became over time.

~

"I cannot believe the demand for our new product!" Mary-Jane gasped over a cup of tea and a chocolate dainty in Mary's pantry with her aunt and Maisie Brown, her new assistant. "I thought we were going to have to usher the queue away half an hour after closing time; suddenly it just seemed to disappear."

"Don't worry, Mary-Jane," Mary assured her. "They'll be back tomorrow bright and early when word flies around concerning your exquisite multi-flavoured dainties, mark my words. People in this area have not been used to the beautiful delights you and Maisie have produced."

"How is everything at your 'new' cottage?" Mary asked Maisie.

"We just can't believe what you have all done for us," Maisie returned. "We have never lived in such a lovely home or such a beautiful area. We love the glorious food you keep providing for us, Missis, never having had to leave the table wi' our bellies full in my recollection, let alone. We would love to live – and work – here with you forever."

She burst into tears, overcome with gratitude and love for these people who had rescued them from a lifetime of degradation and fear.

"All rayt, you buggers!" a harshly guttural voice interrupted the two as its scruffy and dirtily clad body burst into the shop and threatened them with a hefty wooden club. "Empty yon till or else I'll batter yer wi' mi' club!"

The three stopped chattering immediately, fear imprinted on two faces, as Mary stood up to face the miscreant, staring him in the face without either saying anything or moving forward. Looking over his shoulder, she noticed Geoffrey a short way behind the ruffian, pinafore fastened up to the throat and gripping his sweeping broom. As he drew nearer slowly, he said, "Excuse me, sir."

As the roughneck spun round, Geoffrey's broom caught him a resounding crack across the head, felling him with the one blow. Fortunately, his aim had been true because, during the altercation, his eyes had been tightly shut. The attacker's eyes, too, were tightly closed as a result of the broom's accuracy across his – now bloody – skull.

"Well!" Mary-Jane uttered, not quite believing what she had just witnessed. "I didn't expect *that* to happen."

Almost immediately, Geoffrey had rushed out to the back of the shop to alert the local constabulary via his new-fangled telephone. P.C. Arbuthnot and P.C. Jones arrived a few seconds later, largely because the police station was on the corner of their street, literally thirty yards away.

"Cup of tea P.C.s Arbuthnot and Jones, and a slice or two of our best cake?" Mary offered, knowing full well what their unequivocal response would be. "It seems that our miscreant is out for the count."

"We've cuffed him effectively anyway," P.C. Jones replied. "Your generous offer will be gratefully received."

"Any time you are around here," she returned, "don't hesitate to drop in. The kettle is always on the boil and your obviously favourite cake will be plated and ready."

~

"I am not feeling very well because I am expecting," Abigail said quietly at breakfast.

Hal's face dropped out of shock, not because he didn't want a sibling for his Grace, but because he felt like he had been hit by a galloping shire.

"I didn't expect that," he responded, a smile beginning to form slowly. "I thought you felt just a bit under the weather."

"And?" she snapped impatiently.

Hal leaped to his feet and rushed across the room to grasp her in joy, to express his feelings at her news. "I thought we had decided … to just have our little Grace?" he added.

"No choice in the matter, my man," she returned with a shrug and a pained smile. "Nature always has a way of skirting care and any form of protection."

Holding her close and stroking her hair, he experienced a mixture of conflicting emotions – joy at perhaps enjoying similar feelings of elation at producing Grace mark two, and trepidation at the problems that could adjoin such joy. Although not a physician, he still would be able to keep an eye on her progress to production. Probably the best husband to have in such a situation.

"Then we should perhaps call a halt to our professional activities and look after … you," he returned semi-firmly, more as a tentative observation than a direct suggestion.

"We will take it as it comes, if you have no objection," she added quietly with an authoritative air. "Any time my demeanour is compromised, we will postpone whatever occasion is imminent. Are you all right with that, Hal?"

"Whatever you say, my sweet lady," he replied with a smile and a shrug, knowing well the problems a negative answer might cause.

"Daddy?" a tiny questioning voice slid into their conversation. "Had you forgotten?"

Hal turned towards his growing daughter quickly to notice that she had a piece of writing paper and a quill pen in her hands. Her frown told him there was something he had forgotten, and Grace understood straight away from his puzzled eyebrows that he had no idea to what she was referring.

"You said that you would show me how to use this … this feather to write a letter that I could send to Poppy – you do *remember* Auntie Poppy?" Grace went on.

Hal recognised Abigail's expression immediately that Grace had learned to sharp effect. 'Oh dear!' he thought. 'My little urchin is growing into her mother!'

"I'm very sorry my little one," he answered, clapping his right hand to his forehead, which cause Grace to giggle as it always did. "Shall we sit at the dining room's table and do it now?"

Grace clasped his hand in hers as she led him to their favourite 'writing' chairs ready to start her 'feather' lesson.

"Are we going to tell her about Mummy?" Grace asked in a hoarse forced whisper.

"About Mummy?" Hal asked slowly as he glanced at Abigail's grinning face.

"You know…" she muttered in an almost secretive tone. "Mummy and my new little … sister." This caused Abigail to burst into a fit of giggled at the look of shock on her husband's face.

"But … how—?" he gasped in awe.

"How did I know?" Grace said with an air of certainty. "Well, when Mummy says that she is 'expecting', it can mean only one of two things. Either she is waiting for a delivery of goods of some sort, or … she is expecting my new baby sister. I think the appro … approp … proper word is 'pregnant'."

Abigail and Hal looked at each other in shocked amazement. How on earth had she worked that one out?

"How old are you, Grace?" Hal said as he delivered one of his obvious rhetorical questions.

"I'm seven and three quarters, soon to be eight," she responded with a huge sigh. "But you *know* already. Silly Daddy. One of the reasons I want to write to Auntie Poppy, is to arrange a visit to Nice for my birthday. You did promise some time ago. Have you forgotten *again*, Daddy?"

CHAPTER 5

"So, are you telling me that not only do I have a twin sister," Sarah offered, a profoundly puzzled look setting in her unsuspecting Antipodean face, "but I have a brother, too?"

Ross and his fragile wife, Martha, sat quietly on their settee in front of a crackling fire, cups of tea to hand. Although very sad at the blows they had been delivered with the death of their barely seen nipper, they both bore their loss with true Yorkshire stoicism, bearing no outward signs of their grief.

"Small yet unexpected world, eh … Sister?" Ross replied with a welcoming grin.

"I can't believe what's been dropped unexpectedly in my lap," Sarah gasped. "I had no idea that I had siblings let alone a twin sister and a giant for a half-brother."

Martha burst into fits of giggles, releasing some of the pent-up emotions she felt following the loss of her baby boy, George, supported by a huge grin and a comforting arm around her shoulders from Ross.

"Might I ask where my sister is now?" Sarah asked hesitantly. "Would I be able to see her … soon?"

"It would take you the best part of a week were you to embark upon one of the most tedious journeys ever," Ross replied slowly to his sister's frown and shrug. "You see, she lives in the South of France."

"The South of France?" Sarah queried, never having heard of the place. "Where on Earth is that?"

Husband and wife cast disbelieving glances at each other, going on to explain where it was, what she would have to do to get there and how long it would take.

"A week?" she gasped in disbelief. "How…?"

She was interrupted by a banging at the front door.

"Hal and Abigail!" Ross burst out as he opened the door. "How lovely to see you. No Grace?"

"I'm here Uncle Ross!" the young lady uttered loudly as she hurried from the vehicle parked a few yards away, to be picked up and thrown into the air to her squeals of delight.

"Is that a … motor car I see before me?" Ross asked rhetorically as he beckoned the family in, closing the door against the chill.

"Indeed, it is," Hal uttered with pride. "Petrol version of the American Model T Ford."

"How on earth could you afford to buy that?" Martha gasped in shock. "Are you a millionaire?"

"Cost me around about 825 American Dollars," Hal replied with a nod. "Approximately five dollars to the pound, so not *so* bad. The convenience outweighs the cost. The legal speed limit is around twenty-five miles per hour, so it's much quicker than a horse and carriage. And I don't have to feed and provide a warm stable for it."

"Surely not a lot different from a horse?" Martha ventured, a bit of a frown signalling her confusion. "Stables, feed and grooming, I grant you, but … surely you would have to keep the motor able to work so you could make it move and keep it away from bad weather? What *do* you do to make it move?"

"By putting into the tank under the front seat a liquid called 'petrol' that the Americans call 'gasoline'," Hal explained to a blank look on his wife's face.

"I like the smell of pet … er … ol," Grace piped up, to the amused reaction of all present.

In the meantime, Sally, Boulders Wood's new head cook and bottle washer had brought in a fresh tray of steaming tea pot, crockery and slices of sponge cake, that she, with Ross's help, dished out. The look on Grace's face showed her to be in a heavenly place. She loved sponge cake, although at seven and three quarters she was only just getting used to its usual accompanying 'cup of tea'.

"The main reason for our call today is the content of a letter we received from dear Poppy on the Côte d'Azur," Hal began to explain.

"Poppy?" Martha responded, a welcoming smile lifting her spirits. "How is she? Still enjoying the bracing time spent by the Mediterranean Sea?"

"Indeed," Hal added. "Along with her grandfather … and her Aunt Rosie."

At the mention of that name, Sarah's eyes jerked wide as she stiffened in her chair, leaning forward slightly, waiting for the next important words from Hal.

"Perhaps I should introduce our guest," Ross interjected with a smile as he turned towards Sarah. "This young lady is looking for Rosie because she is Rosie's … twin sister, which makes me also her half-brother."

Both Hal and Abigail gasped.

"By the same token, then, they are both Poppy's … aunts?" Hal replied. "Good gracious! Now this world *has* become smaller. You are Rosie's image, even down to your hair colouring and the way you sit."

"Try not to take offence at what my husband is saying, Sarah," Abigail advised. "He says what he sees, noticing even what is most elusive to other people."

"No offence taken," Sarah nodded slowly. "In fact, I need to find her as I have only recently discovered that indeed I *have* a sister, let alone my identical twin."

"Here's the thing," Hal went on, shuffling to the edge of his seat as if he was about to share a secret with her. "The letter we received recently from Poppy who lives with her grandfather, Ross, in Southern France, asked us to collect a significant number of her belongings from the cottage just down the drive from here, and to take them to her on the Côte d'Azur."

"We would then be able to kill two birds with one stone," Abigail added.

"Kill birds because…?" Sarah gasped, a horrified look descending to her face. "Why would you—?"

"It's a saying that originated in the mid-1600s relating to the Greek mythological characters Daedalus and Icarus who supposedly killed two birds with one stone to get enough feathers to make wings to escape from the Labyrinth on Crete," Hal began to explain. "Or Thomas Hobbes is said—"

"Hal!" Abigail interrupted him sharply, a frown warning him not to involve them in his passions. "What he is trying to say is we can cover two goals with the same trip."

"One of those trips would be to take me to see Auntie Poppy in Nice to celebrate the eighth anniversary of my birth," Grace butted in as a reminder for her Daddy Hal. "And the other to take to her what she needs from her cottage."

"I couldn't have explained it better myself," Ross added with a huge grin.

"A question for you Hal, Abigail, and not to forget Miss Grace," Ross said after a moment or two's paying attention to tea and cake. "Would it be possible then for you to take Sarah with you on your journey to Nice? We'll pay for—"

"No need! No need!" Sarah interrupted hurriedly. "My mother – who turns out to have been my true mother's sister – left me a significant amount of cash when she died almost a year ago. So, I am quite able to pay my own way."

"Strange isn't it how wealthy you Australians are?" Hal added. "Rosie is in the same way. So—"

"Hal!" his wife hissed quietly, drawing down her brows in warning not to continue.

"What?" he replied to his wife, spreading his arms wide, genuinely not understanding her warning.

"That's all right. No need to be concerned," Sarah said, smiling widely, dropping to a more serious tone. "When can we go? Tomorrow? My case is readily packed. So, I am … ready … to go."

"Not quite that soon, I'm afraid, young lady," Hal returned with a slight gasp. "We are indeed ready but certain organisational points need to be addressed."

"Timing and tickets," Abigail added, stretching her back to relieve its iniquitously annoying deep-seated ache as her pregnancy had moved on.

"I don't understand," Sarah uttered quietly, a frown invading her tight brows.

"We must decide when we need to go after meticulous research and planning," Hal pointed out. "Only then can we purchase tickets, pack our bags and … catch the … Train Bleu at the start of our adventure."

"I know nothing about any of that," Sarah remarked, almost down-heartedly.

"It will take us at least a week to organise it all," Hal interjected.

"And then?" Sarah asked.

"We will be away at the earliest opportunity," he butted in again. "You have to bear in mind that the train would leave from London to Dover when we would cross the English Channel and travel by another train to Paris. After a day or two's stay to allow exploration of that lovely city, we would catch the Train Bleu to the Mediterranean coast and ... Nice."

"Train Bleu? Mediterranean?" Sarah puzzled almost in panic. "I'm sure it will be very nice, but ... what does it all mean?"

"We have a young lady here with us who has done this several times, who now will explain. Grace?" he finished with a smile.

"But..." Sarah stuttered. "She is only a child."

"I am seven-going-on-eight, if you don't mind," the nipper insisted, almost insulted by their guest's dismissal. "Would you like me to talk it through with you, or not?"

"Did you say you were staying in a hotel?" Ross asked his new half-sister.

"Yes," she agreed in her strong Australian accent. "It's all right, I suppose, but the Grand in Richmond is not my own place."

"Not a good idea ... a young lady on her own," he suggested keenly. "The Grand, you say? Believe it or not, that is where your sister was staying before she came to seek us out. Shall I tell you what I suggested to her?"

"I have really no idea," Sarah replied with her rolling eyes half-shut, not expecting to be tested.

"I suggested that we collect her things, and she should come to stay with us until we could decide—" Ross said with genuine care.

"How and when to get to see Father?" she added.

"You are so sharp, Sister dear," he went on, a hint of gentle sarcasm invading his voice. "She took us up on our offer for her to stay with us. If you would like to do that – stay with your family instead of a load of strangers – we'll go and collect your belongings and—"

"I have them in my suitcase outside this front door," she blurted out quickly, "and I would love to stay here until Abigail and Grace and Hal return to whisk me away to the coat dazzoor."

They all burst into peals of joyous laughter, allowing their newcomer to relax after all her troubles scouring the world for her hidden family. Sighing and sinking back into the settee, a cup of tea and a piece of cake within easy grasp.

Chapter 6

"We've been here before, Mammy, haven't we?" Grace piped up as the train jerked to a halt in Nice's Grand Station. "Do you remember?"

"Indeed, I do, my little one," Abigail agreed with her daughter.

"Do you think my new little sister that you have inside your belly will remember this visit when she is born?" Grace asked to the jerked giggle of her parents.

"Probably—" Hal was about to doubt, to be interrupted by Abigail.

"Most definitely she will," Grace's mum replied very quickly, not wanting to spoil her living in her own imagination.

"I suppose anything is *possible* …" Hal agreed about turning very quickly. It was a good job he had learned to change his views seamlessly so as not to gainsay his wife's opinions. He loved a calm and agreeable life, did Hal.

"I've been about a bit but never seen anything like this," Sarah gasped in amazement at what she saw before her.

"Nothing's changed at all in the station building," Grace observed sagely, almost as if she was about to deliver a resumé of what she had witnessed in her previous visits. "I am very pleased that we haven't come at the time the Mistral blows."

"Miss…?" Sarah said, her wonder at listening to this wizard of an almost-eight-year-old mixing with what had enveloped and overtaken her mind in the time she had been part of her 'new' family. "I don't—"

"Understand?" Abigail interrupted, a half-smile decorating her face at the few times she wasn't wracked with pregnancy pains. "There is most definitely a lot to take in."

"That's why we are here with you," Hal explained. "We've been here before and—"

"Grandpa Ross's motor car!" Grace urged excitedly, jiggling her feet as usual when excitement overcame her. "Over there!"

Poppy and Rosie were already rushing across the pathway leading to the station on the Avenue Thiers, almost as excited as little Grace.

"My goodness!" Poppy gasped as Grace bounced into her arms. "I can see that your age is increasing … along with your weight. When will you be … eight, is it?"

"Very soon," Grace answered with a grin once her feet had regained the floor. "We have a visitor for you."

Sarah had no idea with whom they were dealing, a look of confusion and surprise gathering in her eyes. Once she had set eyes on Rosie, she gasped, not really knowing what to do or say.

"Wonderful to meet you again, Poppy," Hal butted in hurriedly, recognising the dilemma Sarah must have been experiencing meeting two other young women she had never seen before.

"But—?" Sarah gasped catching Rosie's full-on visage as they came face-to-face. "Don't I recog—?"

"Recognise my face?" Rosie interrupted with a grin. "Every day? In the mirror? I am your identical twin, Rosie."

Striding purposefully forward she clasped her sister in a heartfelt clinch that astounded Sarah and almost caused her to collapse with shock.

"So, I *do* have family!" Sarah retorted almost unable to grasp the enormity of what had just happened to her.

"Hello Sarah," a gentle male voice intervened. "Good to meet you at last. I am your *real* father. Welcome to our wonderful family."

~

"But … Family? Everyone?" Sarah asked quietly, still unable to take in the wonder of what she had just experienced. The surroundings of Rosie's apartment with its unbelievable view of the Mediterranean caught her breath as they all sat, teacups to hand, around the significantly enormous balcony. "I understand about you, Father, and my twin and my … niece … Poppy."

"We look on Abigail and Hal and eight-year-old Grace—" Ross began his slow explanation.

"I will be eight *soon*," Grace interrupted, making sure everyone understood that Grandpa Ross had made a slight error in his miscalculation of her age.

"I think he means that you sometimes behave like you are much older than your true age of almost eight," Hal explained as everyone laughed at Grace's serious interjection.

"As far as we are concerned," Ross continued, attempting to mask his grin, "they have been with us and done so much for us that they – you – can't be anything but family, and always will be."

"Does anyone fancy a stroll around the area to familiarise?" Poppy asked with a subdued excitement.

"I think Hal and Grace and I need to refresh and settle

for a little while," Abigail offered with a tired sigh. "Along with little—"

"Georgia!" Grace interrupted quickly as everyone turned to her swift interjection. "I am certain that my little sister will be called … Georgia."

"And why would that be, do you think Grace?" Hal asked, an acceptingly gentle look around his eyes. "I don't think I've ever heard of that name before and so—"

"There is a prince called George, I believe," Grace answered slowly after a bit of thought. "King Edward's son, isn't he? A right royal name. Four King Georges up to now. There has to be a female version of that name. So, I think it must be Georgia. Also, it starts with the same letter as mine, although not the same sound."

An astonished silence descended on the gathering with the adults searching each other's face for an explanation for this astonishing revelation from one so small. Here was a young lady who would go far, especially when her much-awaited sibling appeared on the scene.

"Are you all right, Sarah?" Rosie asked her sister who had been quiet for a while. "You look a little … upset."

"I'm overcome by everything that has happened to me in the last few weeks," Sarah responded quietly slowly. "Until I came to England, I had no idea what family life could be like. I had experienced a lonely and isolated life in the vastness that is Australia as a child, with no-one to play with other than a bunch of sheep. The other children that I knew lived twenty or so miles away and could not be reached other than by horse and carriage, which didn't happen very often. This usually made me think that my mother and I were almost the only people on Earth."

Rosie reached over and drew her unresisting body to her,

understanding how she must have felt. "And now how do you feel?" she asked.

"Overwhelmed but excited to be now in an expanding family in a world without limitations," Sarah's excited face assured them all. "One slight problem though; where do I unpack my case, and where am I going to live – Australia, England or … here?"

"I have a new apartment overlooking the view you see before you that I will be moving into very soon," Rosie assured her. "It could be your new home, too, if you so wished."

"Or would you like to travel the world?" Poppy added with an understanding nod.

"You could even do both, as our Poppy does," Ross interjected quietly. "This could be your base and out there could be the start of your new life, wherever you wanted it to be."

"You mean—?" Sarah queried, settling back in her soft easy chair as her eyes drifted out across the turquoise waters of the Mediterranean Sea.

"Like us, you can afford to do whatever you wish," Poppy suggested. "I will be voyaging to Rome with my book as soon as Hal is ready."

"Hal—?" Sarah puzzled. "Isn't he—?"

"Abigail's husband?" Rosie answered. "Indeed, he is."

"But—" Sarah said, unsure still of relationships.

"He, Abigail and Grace have always accompanied me on the journeys I have undertaken to do book signings," she explained. "I have no idea what is going to happen until their new baby has joined us."

"Would it be possible for the 'Terrible Twins' to journey with you on your next adventure?" Rosie ventured. "We've never been to London, Paris or … New York."

"I've been twice to London and Paris," Poppy added with

a shrug. "But only once to New York. I would never have been to any of them had it not been for Hal and Abigail."

"I would love to go to any of those places," Rosie enthused, rubbing her hands gleefully. "Sarah?"

"Count me in!" she agreed. "Let my – our – new life begin!"

"Then, I must have words with Hal to organise a Grand Tour for us all," Poppy urged with glee. "The Three Musketeers ride again!"

"Are you sure?" Annabel asked, as they arose early enough for George to see to his sheep.

"What?" he returned. "Sure about wanting to get up?"

"About wanting to marry … me?" she replied quietly.

He buttoned his trousers, strode across the bedroom to where she was still lying, put his arms around her and drew her unresistingly soft body to his. He kissed her breasts and lips passionately before reassuring her of his desires.

"I want nothing more," he whispered in her ear. "But I would like to do it quickly and without fuss. Done it twice before and look where that got me. Would that be all right for you?"

"Bring it on as quickly as you want," she sighed deeply. "I want nothing more than to be Mrs George Garside,"

She gasped, a grimace crossing her face as pains began to grow in her lower abdomen, shortly after she heard the closing click of the outside door. George was on his way to his flock of Herdwicks in the north field with no inkling as to his wife-to-be's growing abdominal pains.

How would she be able to cope with these irritants without sharing them with her soon-to-be husband? She had never experienced them before, but then she had not been with child before either. She had become beset with worries with their onset. Were they normal, or did there exist an underlying worrying cause? She winced for a second time as George's sister, Florence, entered, her outer coat shoulders glistening with dampness.

"Annabel?" she queried, a look of concern beginning to decorate her eyes. "You all right?"

"Just a bout of … wind I think," Annabel tried to reassure her. "Pregnancy is not something I have experienced before…"

"George?" Florence ventured.

"Out with his Herdwicks, I believe," Annabel butted in quickly, wanting to change the subject without having to try to explain the fears and feelings she didn't understand.

Chapter 7

"George!" Florence shouted and whistled even more urgently once she caught sight of him amidst his Herdwicks, and he saw her agitated state immediately.

Scattering the sheep, he barged through the not inconsiderable flock leaving his dogs to regroup them, desperate to know what the panic was with his sister.

"It's Annabel," Florence yelled as he drew a little closer to her.

"Annabel?" he butted in sharply only too aware of her condition. "What's—?"

"The doctor is with her," Florence tried to explain. "She collapsed halfway up the stairs in fits of agony. It's a good job we were there and saw what happened."

Without a further word, George turned on his heels and hurried back to the farmhouse, followed by his sister.

"It's a good job we bullied you into having that telephone system installed," Florence warned him as she tried to keep pace with him. Still in silence he rushed up the stairs three at a time, to be met by the doctor leaving the bedroom slowly closing the door behind him slowly and quietly as he rolled down his shirt sleeves.

"Doctor?" George uttered urgently.

"Nothing much I could do. I'm afraid, Mr Garside," the doctor mumbled, putting his hand on George's shoulder as a comforting gesture.

"You mean—" George uttered disbelievingly.

"She's gone, I'm afraid," the doctor reiterated quietly. "The baby boy, too. I've left their bodies on the bed of your spare room upstairs. Perhaps you—"

"Done all that before, doctor, I'm afraid; both parents, two wives and one nipper," George interrupted quietly, eyes welling. "So, I know what needs to be done. I have my four sisters and two brothers-in-law at home to help me."

He fell silent as the doctor closed the outside door behind him, aiming for the Model T Ford motor car that was parked close to one of the empty barns.

Florence slid her arms around her brother once she had finished her telephone conversation with sisters Lilly Victoria and Martha and drew his unresisting body to hers as he dropped his face onto her shoulder. No words were exchanged because they both were aware of the obvious result of such an action.

The creaking stairway drew George's attention from the family gathering in the parlour, not sure what was happening. His face had become ashen and gaunt because of this unexpected shock. Why … did … this … always have to happen to him? The joys that he had experienced gathering about him seemed to have swept away from him unexpectedly and unceremoniously every time.

His daughter, Maisie, the only person he loved remaining in his dour and unproductive life, wouldn't let go of him. *She* didn't want to lose *him* either. She too had lost so much in her short life – a mother, a twin sister and both grandparents. She couldn't allow life to treat her so cruelly anymore.

"We've finished laying her out, George," Lilly Victoria said to the nods of assent from sister Martha as they reached the foot of the stairs. "Mr Jacobs, the undertaker, said he will replace the shell of a coffin with the real one within the next day or two. When that has happened, we'll make sure, with his help, she will be brought into the living room to rest for the next week before the funeral."

George neither moved nor said anything. So much had happened to him over the last year or two that he had hoped a degree of happiness and peace would settle on his shoulders. If only he could feel that happiness that his other siblings and friends had experienced – Lilly Victoria, Martha, Joseph, Ross and … Poppy.

Deep inside, *she* had never left him and never would. This was one of those feelings he would never lose but would have to accept. She was the one he had always loved … and always would, but with no result. Those feelings would always be there, but without hope,

"Would you like us to make all the arrangements, Old Chap?" Ross asked George quietly, understanding the sadness that lay hidden in his friend's heart. "George?"

"Thank you, old friend, but *I* must carry out those last deeds in respect for the woman I was to marry," George insisted. He couldn't allow himself to do otherwise.

"We'll sort all the business out concerning your Herdwicks," Joseph offered, "until—"

"No thank you," George interrupted firmly. "You have enough on your own hands. Besides, I don't have a lot left to do now, so that will be no problem."

"I've spoken briefly to Poppy in Nice, and she has booked space on an overnight train," Ross offered softly. "She'll be back here in four days."

"But I didn't—!" George urged with a frown.

"She insisted," Ross butted in firmly. "Trains allowing of course."

"I know Poppy," Martha added. "I can almost guarantee she will make it in that time."

George's raised eyebrows gave away his deepest feelings to Lilly Victoria. She understood the turmoil churning inside her brother, and she recognised the hopes he had always carried surrounding her. Lilly Victoria hoped they might not surface too much, bolstering her brother's festering desires.

~

"I'll be catching the Train Bleu north-bound soon after midnight," Poppy insisted, much to the chagrin of her grandpa. "That gives me enough time to get back to the North Riding for a short while, before we are back here to start an adventure in Rome with my books."

"About that … adventure," Ross Senior interrupted, a warning tone lacing his words. "We need to talk about the state of that place before you even loosely contemplate setting your precious feet on their soil."

"I don't understand," Poppy puzzled as her grandpa sat next to her on his balcony overlooking the Mediterranean Sea, mug of coffee to hand. "Hal seems to think we should book—"

"A hotel close to the Antica Libreria Cascianelli perhaps?" he went on, seemingly plucking an obscure name out of the air.

"You have me at a loss, Gramps," Poppy responded with a vague shrug.

"The bookshop where you might possibly be having your

signing?" he explained. "Probably the only real bookshop in that country, I should imagine."

"Hal seems to think—" she added, knowing nothing about that shop or even the country it found itself in.

"A difficult country to say the least," Ross tried to explain. "Rough and unformed socially, it can be difficult to get about – unlike Paris and New York."

"How do you know all this?" Poppy asked incredulously. "Have you been there recently?"

"Extended family and … friends either have visited or live there," he assured her.

"Very true," a familiar voice rang out as it entered the balcony. It was Hal, followed slowly by Abigail and Grace. "We need to rethink our proposed visit to Rome for some other time perhaps. Hence the reason our return to New York in a few months to launch your follow-up to *Faithfully Yours*. Abigail tells me it will be in book form reasonably soon."

"New book?" Ross asked, eyebrows raised in anticipation. "You don't hang about, do you? To be called?"

"Not sure whether I should tell you yet," Poppy jested. "Perhaps you should let your excitement build and—"

"*Forever*, by any chance?" Ross offered quietly with a wicked smile.

"And how did you work that one out?" Poppy replied, a surprised raise in her voice. "Hal?"

They all chuckled at Hal's slowly raised shrug and grin. Who else would have known and been able or prepared to share?

"Italy, unfortunately, is still a country in its infancy to some extent," Hal began to explain. "Few natural resources and almost no transportation or industry, the country apparently has a huge national debt, with regionalism still very strong. It needs a year or two yet to be safe enough to do what you did in London, Paris and New York."

"Usual time for the train back to Paris and then England?" Ross asked.

"The funeral for Annabel and her little unborn baby boy is a week from now," Poppy announced quietly and sadly. "Taking tonight's train will get us to Paris within twenty-four hours or so, and then another couple of days or so back to Richmond – allowing for any delays."

"That will give you enough time to pay your respects to the family before the interment," Ross added. "And then what will you do? Prepare for your return journey?"

"Spend time with the family that I haven't done for quite a while," she responded firmly. "I've had enough unexpected family traumas over the last few years that I need to spend time with them."

~

Although stony-faced and quiet, George's emotions at seeing his one-time love within the next few days, bubbled fiercely inside him. He didn't expect in his wildest dreams to see Poppy again. His marriage to Annabel would have seen to that. Why was she coming? Annabel was nothing to her. Dare he hope. Don't be such a fool, lad! Everything that needed to be said about their relationship had been discussed the last time they met.

Surely, they both had accepted that *that* was the last time they would see each other.

Thoughts of the woman he had always loved now filled his mind, and there didn't seem to be any way they could be removed.

Chapter 8

"I still can't get him out of my thoughts," Jenny confessed to her son, Toby. "He is always there, as soon as I wake up, from morning until night."

"I miss him, too," her son agreed. "He could be a bit … unexpected at times, but basically his heart was in the right place."

A deep quiet surrounded them and the comfort he had left them in. Had it not been for his taking hold of their poverty through his 'business deals' and for his unselfishness towards the end, they would never have climbed out of their sorry situation.

"There were times, of course, when we never could see an end to our poverty," Toby went on. "But here we are, comfortable and able to make our way in a difficult world. We owe him everything, and I wish he was here with us now. The only father I ever had.

"Still," he went on after a moment of silence, "he wouldn't have wanted us to be mournful. We have all we need to make our life worthwhile, so we need to get on with it."

"What about George … Garside?" Jenny digressed as her son stood up to put on his overcoat ready for his day's work behind the steering wheel of his luxurious 'taxi'.

"What about him?" he returned, surprised she even knew who he was. "Not our problem. Never has been. I don't intend to pursue issues that were 'Dad's' alone. George Garside never caused me any aggravation, and consequently he will never figure in *my* life. Nor any of his family or associates for that matter."

He finished his cup of tea steadily, ready for his early start to clear the bookings for his taxi that Jonas had provided for him. Did he know what might happen to him at some stage? Had he purposefully provided the wherewithal for them to live a comfortable life when he was no longer there? These questions floated through his sometimes-uneasy mind, not sure what his own reaction should be. By accepting all that Jonas had offered, Toby made sure that his mother would be able to shift their lives in poverty to the past, knowing that she would never have to endure such dreadful living conditions again.

How could this be happening again within such a short space of time? Although George Garside thought he was looking forward to seeing the once most important person in his life, now he wasn't so sure. How would he deal with meeting her in such a relatively short space of time after their parting and her disappearance to almost the other side of the world?

It seemed like the undertaker had become almost part of his extended family with whom he would tread the well-known path to the next world. How many more of his sheep flock would he have to sell to pay for another visit to the graveyard?

"When did you say Poppy would be arriving?" he asked his sister again.

"Six times you have asked that same question," Lilly Victoria responded with a knowing sigh. "She'll be here tomorrow in time for the funeral, and before you ask, she will be staying with us at Boulders Wood after she's spent the first night of her stay at her father's place in Richmond. If she wants to see *you* privately, she'll ask, so don't cause any issues."

"What do you mean, Sis?" he responded, a semi-hurt look growing in his face.

"You know perfectly well what I mean," she pointed out sharply. "She made it quite clear the last time you parted that you had no future together. Wasn't that something to do with the decision you concocted to join with Annabel?"

Point made sharply, he remained silent, accepting the fault for their untimely split. Although he would have preferred that she had stayed, he understood why she hadn't – again another of many mistakes he had made in his handling of their relationship.

Although he would have liked nothing better, he was wary of his deeply buried emotions that his body reminded him still existed. He was sure they would remind him they still lived. However, was he prepared for them to rampage through his consciousness again, perhaps with the same results?

"It might perhaps be a good idea for me not to be here when she arrives," he muttered almost inaudibly.

"You can't do that!" Lilly Victoria urged. "You'll just have to keep your feelings in check … unless Poppy tells you otherwise. You've had to suffer enough heartache with your losses over the last year or two, but there's no need to be extreme. Take things as they come and be sensible."

Her last advice was almost thrown over her shoulder as she snecked the outside door behind her on her way back to her husband and children at Boulders Wood.

Mid-afternoon, the queue of motorised taxis outside Darlington's railway station had virtually consigned horse-drawn carriages to the history books. Mainly varieties of the Model T Ford motor car – or 'Tin Lizzies' as they were affectionately known – they were pushed occasionally into the shade by a much more luxurious-looking machine that offered greater comfort for the travellers who lived further out of town.

Toby's Lanchester Landaulette offered such luxury and comfort to the weary traveller, after the creaking and groaning caused by the carriages' unforgiving metal wheels caressing each twenty-two feet of iron rail.

"Excuse me," a light female voice broke into his daydream of life in a warmer climate.

"Yes, Madam," he replied as he turned sharply to be met by a lovely young, tanned, woman standing next to a travel-worn suitcase. "Do you need a taxi?"

"Yes please," she assured him. "Could you please take me to Dr Spence's surgery in Richmond?"

"Nothing serious, I hope?" he replied with an infectious smile.

"Fortunately, not," she returned. "It's my father's surgery."

"Your name wouldn't happen to be 'Poppy Spence', would it?" he asked slowly.

"It would," she said, smiling equally puzzled. "Have we met before?"

"Unfortunately, no," he countered with a shrug. "However, I notice you have a copy of *Faithfully Yours* in your hand which I have read – twice – and thoroughly enjoyed. Either it's a huge coincidence you bear the same name as the author, or you are—"

"The author?" she interrupted with a giggle.

"How amazing is that!" he continued. "My favourite author riding in my taxi! I have to ask … book number two in the series? Any time soon?"

"The next one is with my publisher – and you can't repeat this to anyone else yet," she whispered conspiratorially, looking over both shoulders. "It is to be called *And Now?*"

"And now I can't wait!" he grinned rubbing both hands together joyfully. "Richmond, here we come!"

"I'm staying overnight with my father, but mid-afternoon tomorrow I shall need a taxi to take me to Boulders Wood Farm," Poppy promised. "You up for that?"

"Two o'clock be all right?" Toby responded without hesitation. "See you then?"

"I was wondering which members of the Royal Family were about to seek my skills as a doctor," Tommy Spence sought from his daughter as she clicked the front door after her. "Lanchester Landaulette? Who on earth can afford to drive one of those?"

"A car hire taxi man," Poppy explained. "The most comfortable carriage/motor car I have ever had the pleasure to ride in, with a very pleasant young man driving it."

"I thought you had become a resident member of the Nice rich," Tommy observed. "To what do we owe the pleasure of your visit?"

"I tried telephoning you a few days ago from Nice but there was no answer," Poppy informed him.

"I had been called out with a colleague to the death of a young woman in childbirth at the Garside farm," he reacted. "Still-born child as well."

"That's the reason I'm here," Poppy returned. "She was George Garside's proposed wife, and I've been invited to the funeral."

"Bit of a long way to come – from the South of France – just for a funeral, isn't it?" Tommy queried, a frown drawing down his brow.

"She was also a friend from when we were twelve," she countered. "I need to pay my respects. Is it all right for me to stay here with you for tonight? I shall need to be off to Boulders Wood late tomorrow afternoon, if that's all right."

"You know the rules, Poppy," Tommy retorted. "Come when you want; stay as long as you wish; depart as and when."

"Once I've done my duty by reacquainting myself with all my former friends – including George – I'll be back here to spend the rest of my time with my family," she rejoined. "Then I will have to be away after a week or so. Ticket booked on the Train Bleu back to Nice."

"Did you travel all that way on your own?" Tommy asked, a slight concern etching his face.

"Came back with Hal, Abigail's husband," Poppy explained.

"Hal, Abigail?" Tommy retorted, unsure of any of his daughter's acquaintances.

"My agents who arrange and attend all my book events," she reacted with a broad smile. "Couldn't manage any of the things I do without them."

"And your next book launch?" he wondered, not sure of where she might be at any time in her new life.

"We are hoping to go to Rome in the near future," she rejoined. "Hal is looking into the feasibility and safety of that country."

"Fortunately, I have no more appointments today, so we'll pack away and head off into the sunset for something to eat,"

Tommy suggested. "Sally is cooking tonight, if that's all right with you."

CHAPTER 9

"Stop mekkin such a lot o' noise!" a gruff voice whispered as quietly as it could to its companion. "Thas off ter weck somebody up."

The two ruffian burglars shuffled about in the downstairs office at the back of the house, trying drawers and cupboards in their attempts to find … something of value.

A sharply creaking cupboard door hinge drew the house's occupant from his shallow sleep, aware that he and his mother weren't alone in their comfortable property. Reaching over to the side of his bed, he picked up a hefty club from the floor as he slid silently from his rest. Knowing perfectly well where the intruders were, he shadowed the walls silently down the stairs ready to remonstrate with them, weighty club to hand.

Having worked out from their movements how many there were, he had decided he would be able to tackle effectively at least one of the two.

Unable to sustain the hefty blow that a club to the side of the head wrought upon him, the larger of the two miscreants collapsed in a heap next to a large mahogany sideboard, a pool of blood gathering about his head slowly. Shocked to hear his partner's thud to the wooden floorboards, the second of the two burglars froze in fear that the same might happen to him.

"A sensible decision," Toby retorted with a satisfied smile. "Now, if you'd be so good as to let me know who sent you and why you are rifling through our belongings. It's not money you are after because we haven't any. Priceless artifacts, perhaps? Something that will fetch a glorious life-changing price, maybe?"

"Hello, hello, hello," a deep voice sounded from the doorway just behind Toby, causing him to step to one side and look around, club ready to re-use. "It's all right, sir, no need to use your self-defence guard again. We are from the police station just around the corner. Constables Harris and Green. We'll take over from here, if you please."

"Constable Harris? Thank goodness!" Toby gasped. "But how—?"

"We happened to be passing your – open – back doors, and seeing tale-telling flickering lights, we thought it might be worth a look, and how right we were!" the constable explained. "Constable Green has hurried back to the constabulary to summon a Black Maria to transport these two miscreants back to a cell to answer one or two questions."

"What about—?" Toby asked.

"The sleepy one? He'll wake up no doubt with a bit of a headache," the policeman suggested. "Please check through your belongings to see if anything has been taken. I should be obliged if you'd let us know your findings."

⁓

"And what was all that noise about in the early hours?" Jenny Bott asked her son at breakfast. "You coming back in after a night out with your friends?"

"What friends?" Toby queried, a frown displaying his lack of understanding. "When was the last time I went out with … friends? You knew the only friend I ever had is no longer with us. Unfortunately, he wasn't my father, but we were close enough for me to consider him a good friend.

"I love the fried breakfast you cook for me," he went on after a moment or two of quiet. "We could afford to employ someone to do it for us, you realise?"

"The noise? This early morning?" his mother went on, returning to their original conversation.

"A couple of dumbheads decided to break in and scour the office to find something worth selling," he responded dismissively. "Opportunists, obviously. The only things worth anything ever to be kept in there were the two envelopes of cash Jonas Jamieson gave to us. You put yours in the bank and I use mine to run the taxi."

"You never knew about this, then?" she returned, reaching into her handbag to draw out a package, drawing a scowl and a slight inclination of the head from her son.

He opened it very carefully to find a fist-sized box. He took off the lid to discover inside – much to his shock – a rather large glinting, cut stone that looked like a diamond.

He frowned again and shrugged, at a loss what to say.

"I may be stating the obvious," he muttered, "but this can't be—"

"A rather large diamond," she replied quietly with a nod. "It is real, and I found it in one of the hidden drawers in the sideboard. I think you need to sit down before I tell you how much it is worth."

He sat back down at the table, a very unsure look gathering on his face as she took back the stone.

"At 5 carats, apparently, it is worth at least twice as much as the house we are living in," she stated quietly. "It seems like *that* is what your 'dumbheads' must have been looking for."

***

"Can I assume that you don't live locally?" Toby asked Poppy as he headed for Boulders Wood behind the steering wheel of his taxi.

"No," she responded thoughtfully having enjoyed her quick visit to her father's family home. It was very difficult to leave, and perhaps she needed to visit more often wherever in the world she was based. At least a couple of weeks twice a year sounded about right. "I live in Nice."

"Nees? And where in the world is that?" he questioned with a smile. "These best-selling authors, eh? I'm afraid that not only have I never been there, I have never been outside of this area. My mother and I have been very poor for most of our life."

"Then how come you have such a magical motor car?" Poppy asked, quite taken aback by his pronouncements. "Father Christmas?"

"My stepfather, who passed away not long ago, left us enough to manage on – including this wonderful motor car," he carried on as he steered his way along Boulders Wood's noisy driveway. "Here we are. My! What a wonderful place."

"Thank you for the ride," Poppy said after paying his fare.

Giving her a piece of paper in return bearing his telephone number for the next time she was in the area, he turned the motor car around and slowly crunched his way back to Richmond, a satisfied smile on his face for having spent time with such a beautiful young lady.

"Poppy!" Ross greeted his niece with joy drawing her to him in a welcoming hug as she closed the porticoed door behind her. "Long time no see. Glad to be back?"

"It seems like I've never been away," she retorted with a cheeky grin. "Unfortunately, the weather here is nowhere near as good as on the Côte d'Azur."

"Your grandpa? How's he managing?" Ross asked, keen to know how his father was managing on his own without Nell.

"He's at a loss most of the time but being kept on his toes by a granddaughter and twin daughters around him most of the time," Poppy explained. "He still misses Nanny Nell though, more than he lets on, I am sure."

"His chest condition any better?" Ross returned quietly.

"He seems to be managing within the climate that the Mediterranean affords him," she reacted. "I don't think he will be coming back here any time soon."

"We've probably seen him for the last time, then," Ross answered, a sad tone in his voice. "Much as I would love to, I can't afford to spend time away from the farm to visit Southern France. C'est très difficile."

"Hark at you! French blood flowing through your veins," Poppy acknowledged with glee.

"Learned that when Joseph and I went to Mother's funeral," Ross said, pushing out his ample chest in fun.

How many more times is this going to happen? George's mind slurred through this cold and drizzly dark Thursday morning in February. His memories of a similar day a relatively short time before, slid painfully into his mind; his first wife, Alice, followed none-too-long after by his second, Florence. Same graveyard, same sort of time. Two wives followed by a near-ly-wife on a rainy and cold day.

When was he going to learn that's it's not possible to fill a space that's not meant to be filled? He knew as well as anyone else that he wasn't meant to marry again, especially when his 'new' wife was expecting someone else's child. Did he never learn?

Here he stood, forlorn, bare headed in the cold drizzle, watching the coffin descend slowly into what seemed like a never-ending black abyss. He couldn't believe the mistakes he had made and had been forced to reconcile over an open grave on a grim day such as this.

Selfish in the extreme, wishing for someone – anyone – to stand resolutely by his side as his forever partner, whether wife or not, he couldn't stop those feelings of regret and loss filling his emotions to overflowing.

"We therefore commit this body to the ground … earth to earth…"

How well he understood those grim words!

Unaware of a set of eyes settling on his bowed head from barely ten yards behind him, he wrapped himself in his unshared grief without realising his one true love was drawing in his metaphorical grief to herself. Poppy had travelled non-stop for four days to be with him. Unaware of that in his self-imposed isolation, he might as well have been there on his own.

"Poppy!" he gasped as the gathering separated to go its own way after the service. "I didn't expect—"

"Couldn't not be here, George," she explained. "After all, she had been *my* friend as well – for a time at least."

"Look," he added, embarrassed to be making excuses as he turned away to make his way back to the farm. "Lot to see to. See you before you return to the sun?"

Then he was gone. Another friendship cast onto the refuse heap.

Aghast and very disconsolately shocked, she caught up with her Uncle Ross, whose surprised face said it all.

"Not the same George that you knew of old, I'm afraid," he offered as they walked back to Boulders Wood and refreshments for the family.

CHAPTER 10

"Whatever possessed him to decide to marry Annabel?" Poppy asked quite naïvely. "She walked away from him before, probably realising how persuadable he would turn out to be, despite his apparently brusque nature."

"As we all know, George never sees how situations can play out," Ross ventured. "The number of times he has made an obviously dodgy decision to have it come back to bite him in the nether regions! He always seems to make such decisions to regret them quite soon after. You and he are just such a case."

"Ross!" his wife, Martha, interjected, her tone warning him that *that* was not a good example to choose.

"It's all right, Martha," Poppy responded with a slightly painful grimace. "That I know, much to my chagrin. Partly my fault for not handling his responses as well as I might have done. I still think a good deal about him."

"Well," Martha returned, changing the direction of their conversation, "it is wonderful to have you here. Any chance of you returning on a permanent basis? We do miss you. Little Annie here also would love to be able to spend time with you."

"Auntie Poppy is ear," Martha and Ross's daughter burst into the conversation.

"Auntie Poppy is *here*, my little sweet," Martha corrected her two-year-old daughter with a smile.

"I won't be coming back permanently … I don't think," Poppy responded seriously. "I could be persuaded, however, to drop in a little more frequently, in between the book signing events I intend to hold in different countries."

"Do you really want to continue wasting time telling your wishy-washy stories?" Ross asked apparently seriously.

"Ross!" Martha warned him. "That's definitely not your opinion on Poppy's skill and mindset!"

"I know he is having me on," Poppy laughed as she threw a white cotton serviette at her uncle playfully.

"In fact," she explained, "I have had many requests from avid readers to hurry up with my follow-ons to *Faithfully Yours*."

"And?" Ross asked seriously, because, having read the original story, he, too, wanted to see where it was going.

"Launch of *And Now?* to be at our original book shop in Richmond … in a few weeks' time," Poppy said, a frisson of excitement surrounding her body. "Followed by London, Paris and New York over the next month or two."

"New York again?" Martha remarked. "Quite a way to travel?"

"A fantastic experience!" Poppy enthused with a seriously excited look gathering about her face. "Except for one disturbing incident…" she went on, explaining the steps taken by Abigail with a ruffian's interruption of business.

An urgent knocking on the outside front door drew their attention quickly to who was desperate to see them.

"Sounds important," Poppy said, giving a quizzical look at the occupants of the front room. Turning sharply to see who had been let in, she was startled to see…

"Hal?" she said, surprised by the unexpected appearance of her friend.

"Just had a call on the telephone from Ross Booth in Nice," he said almost matter of fact without any emotion. "Abigail has been taken into hospital and has delivered our baby very prematurely. Abigail is all right, but they are not sure about Georgia."

"Georgia?" Ross queried. "I thought she was called Grace?"

"Grace is our older daughter," Hal corrected. "'Georgia' was to be the name of our new arrival … named by … Grace. Shall you be coming back with me Poppy?"

"Of course I will," Poppy returned without hesitation. "When?"

"There is a train to London tomorrow afternoon that will allow us to catch the Train Bleu the late evening of the following day," Hal explained. "Allowing us to be back in Nice within a touch over four days."

"We need to—" Poppy replied after a few moments of thought.

"Already done," he replied quickly.

"Is this some sort of a code, or thought transference, or…" Martha queried. "Only—"

"I know Hal of old," Poppy answered with a chuckle. "What he is saying is that he has already booked the seats on both trains. So, all I need to do is to pack."

"What about getting a lift to the railway station?" Hal suggested on the late morning of their return to Southern France. Hal, of course, was eager to return to Nice to find out how his wife was progressing, and whether he *had* another daughter. He had had no further communication as to whether Georgia had joined – and remained with – her potential sister, Grace. Only time would tell.

"Taken a leaf out of your book, my dear Hal," Poppy responded with a wide beam.

"And that means?" he returned, not quite understanding what she was saying.

"A saying that was first used in the early 1800s," she assured him. "It means I have done something that you would have done, and in this case what you suggested has already been organised. In fact, if I'm not very much mistaken, I can see and hear his approach up the driveway now."

"Weren't your father and mother—?" Hal started.

"Stepmother," Poppy interrupted with a benign smile.

"Weren't your father and stepmother disappointed that you are having to leave so soon?" Hal went on.

"No," Poppy explained. "They know I will visit at some other time. Besides, they have a couple of young children to keep them occupied as well as a very busy medical surgery to look after."

A very shiny and expensive-looking motor car drew to a halt close to them.

"This is our taxicab ready to start us on our journey home," she continued.

"Wonderful!" Hal exclaimed excitedly. "I've never been inside a Lanchester Landaulette before, although I know of them and their sheer opulence. A taxi, eh?"

"Good afternoon, Mistress Poppy," the taxi driver greeted her as he drew his motor to a sedate halt at the top of Boulders Wood's driveway.

"Good afternoon, Master Toby," she replied with a satisfied smile. "Thank you for being here on time."

"It is my pleasure, I have to say," Toby responded. "We

have plenty of time to enjoy the drive to the railway station."

Upon the taxi's arrival, Hal's face took a warily stern look with eyebrows warning of something troubling him. This he maintained throughout the journey to Middlesbrough's railway terminal. Although Poppy had noticed the change in Hal's demeanour, she said nothing about it until they had dismounted the taxi and paid what was owed to its driver.

"You do know who the taxi driver is, I assume?" he broached to her as they boarded the train for London.

"A pleasant young man who drives comfortably well and provides a beautifully planned and carried out service," she replied openly. "Are you about to tell me he is the devil incarnate?"

"Not far away," Hal begun to explain. "He is the stepson of the anathema to this family that is – was – Jonas Jamieson, although I am not aware that he perpetrated any harm or ill wishes on anyone else in this world."

"He has always done what he promised to me," she added. "Providing comfortable rides in his taxi at a reasonable cost."

"It would be wise to keep an open mind," Hal advised.

"I shan't be seeing him for at least another six months," she said. "Then what could he do from the seat of a moving motor vehicle?"

"You would be surprised," Hal finished. "Just be mindful whenever – if ever – you see him again. Train's in and our first-class seats beckon. Shall we away?"

"Indeed, my thoughtful guardian," Poppy said with a smile, linking his arm with hers as they made their deliberate way to their reserved carriage. "Our next adventure begins within the next ten minutes."

CHAPTER 11

George sat on his own in the front room at Garside Farm. Not knowing which way to turn for solace, his mind had turned blank with no comfort from anywhere or anyone. Three partners had been spirited away along with two parents and one child, not to mention the foetus Annabel was carrying. He had all his siblings available to comfort him – four sisters – but none of them was close, either mentally, emotionally or physically. Alone in a black tunnel, he did not know what to do.

The one person that could have provided comfort and closeness was there at the funeral, but she could not, did not approach him because he could not face her, following their recent history.

Totally, completely and utterly … alone.

———

"What are we going to do about our George?" Charity asked of her sisters, knowing the answer she would perhaps receive, as they drank tea and ate sandwiches at Boulders Wood.

"Unfortunately, he never listens to common sense and almost always makes the wrong decisions which trundle him along the wrong path," Lilly Victoria responded, speaking for them all. "Whatever we say, he will neither listen to nor act upon."

"Where is he now, instead of being here with his family, being looked after by folks that care?" Charity offered with a shrug. "I know it needn't be said, but his one true love that would have happily married him, he rejected until it was too late."

"Ever since childhood he has been the same," Florence iterated firmly. "Always unable to make rational decisions that meant anything. His one main fault? He would never take advice that would allow him to make progress in his private life. Classic case? Moving out of the partnership with Boulders Wood and bringing in … sheep. Although I know little about running a modern farm, I would personally have remained in the partnership with the McIntyres."

"What we need to do now, as opposed to destruction, is to support him as much as we are able," Ross added, reiterating the opinions he shared with George from when he took over the Garside Farm upon his father's death. "Although I feel sure it may not count for much, I will talk to him about the farm's future."

"If we don't, I fear it will close down and disappear," Joseph agreed. "The way farming is moving now gives me no hope for a positive outcome. We in this farm are finding significant difficulties competing with all the other farms in our area. Sheep farming on its own is not the way forward. We were beginning to see progress when the two farms were in partnership."

"The two types of animal farming have always been separate – having cows and sheep in the same field never worked," Ross explained. "Because the two animals cropped grass in very different ways, most sensible farmers didn't do it."

"Having said that though," Joseph pointed out, "I have heard of some that do use the same grazing fields."

"Probably because they have much less land than we do," Ross agreed. "I still feel we could have made a success of what we had planned to do before the two farms parted."

"I have certainly seen a downturn in our finances since we went our separate ways, as did George the last time we talked," Joseph put forward, quoting George's opinion about his farm's progress. "I certainly think it would be useful to reconsider the position of our two farms."

<hr>

The open log fire cracked and spat, its garish yellow tongues lighting only the chimney back, the hearth, and the knees of the lone figure sitting in his favourite chair. The occasional flicker of largely motionless, half-open eye lids betrayed the unconsciousness of the chair's occupant.

"So that's where you are," Florence uttered disdainfully, becoming aware of her brother as she entered the front room, with his daughter's limp and unconscious body cradled asleep in his arms.

"Don't worry," she went on, a hint of sarcasm decorating her words as she crossed the room towards the stairs, "I'll put Maisie to bed."

"You still there George?" Florence asked flippantly as she re-entered the sitting room once Maisie had been tucked up in her bed. "George? Are you listening to me, George?"

Realising that his lack of response seemed to be unintentional, she strode across to his favourite chair to address him face on. She wasn't about to allow him to ignore her words. Shaking him to try to draw his attention, she realised he was unable to respond because he was unconscious and had been so for a considerable amount of time.

In a state of panic, feeling that her brother might be close to death, she grabbed the telephone to alert their local doctor.

***

"Reasonably commonplace in someone as busy as your brother, I'm afraid," Dr Twist explained. "It's a condition that was recognised many years ago by Hippocrates, the father of modern medicine, that he called 'apoplexy', which means in Greek 'struck down by violence'."

"What does that mean?" Florence asked with a serious frown. "Is it something that can be … cured?"

"Recent findings discovered that this condition can be linked to something that has disrupted the blood supply in the person's brain," the doctor replied. "It can, of course, lead to disability or even … death.

"Hopefully in George's case that won't happen, probably because we have caught the problem in time," he went on after a few minutes' pause to replace his coat and to fasten his medic's bag of tricks. "The new-fangled motor ambulance will have him in hospital in no time at all."

"What's happening here?" Sister Charity asked as she came in from the gathering at the McIntyres' place. "Why is there an ambulance just chugging its way to what I gather is the local hospital, and where is George?"

Florence explained what the doctor had just told her, much to Charity's shock and horror.

"Could he … die?" she gasped. "Good God! This family! Shouldn't we go to the hospital to see what's happening?"

"The doctor said it wouldn't be necessary, and, of course, we have Maisie to look after," Florence pointed out as she flopped into George's chair. "We're the only family she's got if he doesn't … come back. It's possible he's been hit by something called a 'stroke'."

Immediately she burst into a fit of sobbing, realising how unpleasant she had been to her brother, even though he wouldn't have heard a word she had hissed at him. She could only hope he *hadn't* heard her!

"You stay here then," Charity suggested to her, "while I nip over to speak to our Lilly Victoria and Martha and perhaps ask if they can take Maisie in the morning to be with *their* nippers until we find out about our George."

~

"Not long now, Hal," Poppy noted as the Train Bleu, which had turned out to be a Train Vert in Paris with much less comfortable accommodation for their overnight voyage, made a joltingly unpleasant stop at each station en route. "Nice next stop."

"Thank goodness for that," Hal observed. "That was one of the most unenjoyable journeys I have had the misfortune to suffer anywhere in the civilised world. 'Green Train' indeed!"

With their window open as the rickety engine slowed on its entry to their destination station, the sea air wafted into their carriage on a warm breeze that almost took away the discomfort they experienced during the last few hours of non-sleep.

Looking out towards the Mediterranean Sea from the railway station's foyer, Hal tried to catch sight of his waiting wife, but to no avail. Having given premature birth a few days ago, it was highly unlikely that she would be there. Would Ross Senior be waiting in his motor car to pick them up? Again, unlikely. Still, the apartment was only a few yards away from where Hal and Poppy now were, so they decided to get the use back in their legs by walking. Good, quick exercise, and …

they would be in line for a cup of tea and a bun more quickly.

"Anybody home?" Poppy shouted as she knocked on her grandpa's front door.

"No answer?" Hal asked somewhat impatiently.

"Don't forget that it's quite a long walk from the veranda to the front door," Poppy said with a grin at the funny she had just used. There was no response from Hal, however. Sometimes his sense of humour just … didn't … exist.

"Hello you two," Rosie's very recognisable voice greeted them once she had opened the door. "Don't just stand there. Come in. The kettle is singing its heart out on the stove ready to make you a cup of tea."

"No Abigail?" Hal noticed, a slightly panicky tone in his voice.

"Still in hospital, I'm afraid," Ross advised him. "Very much waiting to see you. Cup of tea and then off for a ride in a motor car?"

"Hal doesn't do cups of tea when he is … concerned," Poppy explained. "But I do."

"How are things with you then Grandpa?" she went on.

"Probably little different from the last time we were together … about a week or so ago," he replied with a slightly wicked smile. "Still missing Nell of course. Loving having my daughters and granddaughter around me. Lucky chap that I am. Both Rosie and Sarah now have apartments hereabouts and appear to be settled – similar sort of climate to the one they left in Australia, but a bit less arid."

"I don't see Sarah," Poppy noted. "Not gone back—?"

"Certainly not!" Rosie interrupted quickly. "Out with … friends."

Ross smiled at the disdain he noted on her face at the mention of his daughter's 'friends'. Not his cup of tea either.

"Afternoon tea anybody?" Rosie asked as she deposited a gilt-edged tray loaded with white China crockery and home-baked buns and fruitcake.

"Well, I might just…" Hal said quietly as he reached out for a piece of fruitcake and – unusually for him – a strong … cup of tea, a smile returning to his face.

C H A P T E R   1 2

"I thought we might sell this house and move to some-where less … obvious," Jenny Bott offered her son as he locked the front door behind him. "We could perhaps sell the diamond and—"

"And what?" he responded with a frown. "Get half as much as it's really worth? And then?"

"I don't know," she hissed. "Move to a smaller house in the country, perhaps?"

"I don't think so," he insisted. "What we need to do is to deposit the stone in the bank for safety to allow its value to increase, and then sell up and move to Southern France, may be?"

"Southern France? Where's that?" she puzzled, knowing nothing about anywhere that wasn't … here.

"For a start, it's much warmer than here, allowing you not to need external heating," he muttered. "I believe also it's close to the sea, though I have no idea really where that might be."

"The thing I'm worried about is coming home one day and finding the same people rummaging through our belongings looking for money or goods that can be exchanged for money," she went on. "If you're not here and I'm on my own…?"

"Hmm," Tobby muttered quietly to himself. She had a point there. If they forced their way in while she was on her own because he was at work, she could be hurt or even … killed, knowing that these sorts of thugs have no compunction about making sure they are not disturbed. It wouldn't be just a case of moving two streets away. It would have to be somewhere they couldn't be found; somewhere not in this country, perhaps.

"Abigail," Hal whispered quietly as he settled in a chair next to his wife who seemed to be asleep in her hospital bed. He wanted desperately to draw her body next to his but didn't want to wake her.

"Better not disturb her, Mr McIntyre," an English-speaking nurse advised. "She's had precious little rest and—"

"I'm awake," a quiet, tremulous little voice interrupted their conversation. "Hal?"

"I'm here my sweet," he replied slowly, only just loud enough for her to be sure it was her husband.

"And before you ask, I'm feeling sore and very tired," she went on, eyes still tightly closed. "We lost little James, I'm afraid." Tears began to ooze onto her cheeks as desperation took over.

Hal didn't know what to say because he hadn't ever seen his new little son, but he tried to slide his arm under her stiff body nonetheless, to groans because of her injuries brought about through what he thought was an unproductive pregnancy.

"James has gone," she reiterated, "but … Georgie is being looked after by the nurses in a special ward close by."

"But … Georgie?" Hal puzzled, shocked by what he thought he was hearing. "You don't mean—?"

"I gave birth prematurely to twins," Abigail whispered, opening her eyes slowly to gaze into his. "James didn't make it, but Georgie did. He's very under-sized but is reasonably healthy nonetheless."

"I need to rest now," she went on, eyes fast shut again after a few minutes of silence.

Realising there was nothing he could do, feeling emasculated and useless, he looked at the nurse who indicated perhaps he ought to leave her to rest.

"Perhaps later in the day tomorrow might be a sensible time to revisit," the nurse advised. "You should be able to see your son then too."

Turning on his heels, he made his way out of the ward as if in a different world of make-believe, unable to comprehend what he had just learned.

"Hal?" Poppy reacted as he approached her in the hospital waiting area.

He stopped quickly, brought to an unexpected halt by her tone, as if he wasn't expecting her to be there. Looking into his almost shocked face she saw a distant but concerned frown that she had rarely seen in all the time she had known him; unresponsive and apparently not seeing her though he seemed to be looking her in the eyes.

"Are you all right, Hal?" she asked again, finding it very hard to get through to him. "Abigail? Hal?"

Finally registering that someone that knew his name was trying to hold a conversation with him, Hal shook his head vigorously as if trying to reconnect all his senses that had become disconnected since trying to converse with his wife.

"Poppy?" he queried, not sure. "It seems like I have gained a son and lost a ... son."

"Not sure what you mean," she said quietly shaking her

head slowly. "Lost … yet … gained?"

"Abigail, unbeknown to us, must have been carrying twins, but her premature birthing took one away," Hal tried to explain rather slowly with a deep frown. "Although it seems like one of them survived the trauma. Not seen him yet but apparently, he's a little boy called Georgie. Decided upon by Grace, I believe.

"Abigail's absolutely worn out and needing sleep and a good deal of rest," he went on after a little pause. "Never seen her so … tired."

"Shall we away back to grandpa's place and have some tea?" Poppy suggested. "You must be starving. I am."

Their walk back to the apartment was undertaken in silent thought. Hal kept his face down, watching his feet every step of the way, even though the sea drew Poppy's gaze, along with a warm zephyr-like breath across their face. Once inside, Hal made for Grace straightaway; to sit by her bed remembering in his head the day *she* entered this world.

When he was satisfied she was at rest, he joined Poppy and her family around the veranda table to partake of a sandwich or two, a piece of chocolate gâteau, and a glorious mug of hot tea.

Questions about Abigail's condition prompted general responses from Hal concerning when they ought to be back at the hospital. He knew his wife would need time to recover, along with premature Georgie, allowing them both sufficiently to achieve normality by being released from their captivity in a French maternity hospital.

～

"I don't care how you do it, but the stone needs to be recovered from where it is now hiding," the Big Boss hissed at his henchmen through gritted teeth. "Do you realise how many thousands of guineas will fall into our lap should you find it? The key to this problem is Jonas Jamieson."

"But he died on his settee with my knife growing out of his chest," one of the gang urged.

"Ah but did you ask him where he had hidden it before you thrust that blade into his body?" Big Boss asked sarcastically. "And he is now six feet beneath the turf with that secret still within his head."

"But—" Gangman protested, to be slapped down, physically and mentally. "'Arry was flattened the last time his house was 'examined' and Terry was arrested by the local constabulary. So where do we go from here?" Gangman complained.

"Just my point, idiot," Big Boss declared, his foul stale breath pouring over Gangman's rough stubbly face. "*You* have to find a way to search without getting caught, and if you find nothing, get some answers from the young lad of the house and his mother."

"He's bound to be wary now," Gangman argued. "So—"

"Keep a watch to see when he leaves, and the same with his mother," Big Boss snarled. "They don't have staff that live in the house, so there's bound to be a time when it's empty. Go on! Get on and do something about it. If you don't find the stone soon, you could be sorry."

His threat was palpable that the whole gathering believed. Big Boss never reneged on any of his threats, carrying them out to the letter should he be disobeyed.

"What is this stone thing when it's at home?" Brainlack asked Gangman once they had left Boss Man to his threats.

"I think it's some sort of a precious jewel that was stolen from the Crown Jewels or somewhere," Gangman hazarded a wild guess. "He thought Jonas Jamieson had lifted it from the stash taken from Thresher Hall a while ago – one of the reasons why Jamieson found my blade in his heart."

"Well, I know that the lad we are talking about, and his ma won't be in the property this afternoon," Brainlack said quietly, touching the side of his nose with his forefinger and looking over his shoulder at the same time to make sure that no-one was eavesdropping.

"And how on earth would you know that?" Gangman hooted, just short of calling him a liar.

"More useful contacts than you could possibly know about, Gangman," Brainlack threw back at him, pulling himself up to his full six feet five inches in height as he looked down on the much shorter and older gang member.

"Either we do this together, or I will take it to Boss Man and do myself what he asks," Brainlack threatened without fear of reprisal from him.

"This afternoon, then," Gangman agreed, realising how much his compatriot had over him that could be used against him. He would have to plan how he could use the afternoon so that he wouldn't be at a disadvantage.

~

"How is it that one of the premature twins died and the other did not?" Rosie asked, puzzled about this unexplained conundrum.

"France is the world leader in this field, I have to tell you," Ross began to explain. "In the late 1800s, a chap called Étienne Stéphane Tarnier and his assistant, Pierre-Constant Budin, recognised the importance of a warm, humid environment and high standards of hygiene for premature babies, and they went on to invent what they called 'incubators' for premature babies to spend their important early days in. The first incubator, or 'isolette' as it was called in France, was simply a wooden box with an air vent and a hot water bottle inside. The box had a glass lid so the baby could be viewed."

"So, Abigail is lucky to have had her babies in France?" Sarah queried.

"The first country to provide nursing care and medical treatment for premature babies – a world leader in neonatology," Ross explained.

"And what does … neonatology mean?" Sarah went on to ask.

"Two Latin words – 'neo' meaning new and 'natal' meaning birth," he added. "Many doctors before the late 1800s didn't consider premature babies worth saving, with very little concern for what they called 'weaklings'. Fortunately, Hal and Abigail's weakling Georgie was born here."

"Whereas his twin brother didn't survive," Rosie pointed out forcefully.

"One of those things, I'm afraid," Ross insisted. "It was not meant to be."

"Where did this Tarnier person get the incubator idea from?" Rosie went on.

"Possibly from knowing of and watching little chicks being cared for in them?" Hal suggested as he joined the group.

"My little Georgie is being cared for in one as we speak," he went on, sipping the hot tea that had been provided for him. "Just seen him through his little glass roof. Lifesaver, I have to say."

"How is Abigail?" Poppy asked, concerned about her friend.

"Finding it hard not to be able to suckle her baby, and even harder to come to terms with the loss of his twin brother," Hal replied, downcast as the thoughts of Little James floated into his head. "Georgie is being fed artificially through a tube with sterilised cow's milk. 'Gavage' they call it."

"Gracious me!" Rosie gasped, to Poppy's knowing smile. "How do you know all this?"

"He knows because he is … Hal McIntyre," Poppy explained with an arms-out shrug. "He knows … everything."

Chapter 13

"What are you doing Mr Garside?" Nurse Grieves said to George as she found him standing by his bed. "You shouldn't be out of your bed at this time."

"I can't stop 'ere any longer," he mumbled almost as if he didn't know what he was saying. "Mi sheep and mi daughters need me. I can't do wi' liggin abaht all day. Mi clows? What's tha done wi' mi clows?"

"Clows, Mr Garside?" she replied, a puzzled frown etching her face.

"Aye, tha knows," he insisted. "Shirt, trousers, booits – clows."

"Mr Garside," Dr Twist greeted his patient as he sidled through the ward double doors on his way to visit. "Should you be up so soon?"

"An' oo are you?" George muttered, not recognising the doctor he had met at home on many an occasion because of his visits to attend to daughters and parents. "Do I know thee?"

"Aye, tha does, lad," Dr Twist responded in like dialect as he too was a Yorkshireman born and bred. "I've sin to thee and thi family on many an occasion. Ahm tellin' thee that tha needs to get thissen back into thi bed coz tha's not well enough to be aht."

Shocked to hear what he had to say and how he said it, George froze, not knowing what to do or how to do it. The doctor took hold of his wrist and guided him back to where he needed to be, beckoning the nurse to cover him with the sheets he had just relinquished, and to tuck him in. Almost immediately his eyes closed, and he started a degree of heavy breathing.

Within seconds the ward door opened, allowing sisters Lilly Victoria and Martha to enter.

"Just the people I need to see," the doctor said with a sigh.

"Dr Twist?" Lilly Victoria said puzzling why he might be here. "Can I assume you are here to see our brother?"

"Indeed, I am," he responded, starting to recount the conversation he had just held with George.

"I am hoping it's just a phase that he can't remember and which won't return," he finished explaining. "He's sleeping now and hopefully what just transpired won't happen again."

"Perhaps one of us needs to be with him during all visiting times?" Martha suggested. "We have enough family members to cover the whole week."

"I think that's a good idea," the doctor agreed. "Just so he has familiar faces surrounding him that can talk him back to doing what he needs to do. The brain can do strange things where a stroke has been involved."

"We understand," Lilly Victoria added as she and her sister sat down, one either side of the bed. "We remember our mother's last days very well."

Nodding, the doctor turned and strode out of the ward, leaving the two sisters to discuss what they had just encountered.

"I hope it's nothing … permanent," Martha said haltingly.

"If it is, that could be our George done for."

"We'll have to give it time and ... hope for the best," her sister returned. "Otherwise ... he might tread the same path as Mother."

"Nar then," Brainlack muttered as he squeezed his way under the low doorway into the back room of Jenny Bott's house in Richmond. This was just too easy for words, but it would stand him in good stead in his dealings with Boss Man were he to hand over his prize stone that he so desperately wanted. "This first drawer in the sideboard should do the trick."

"Get him!" a loud voice filled the room and shocked Brainlack into immobility while three sets of very strong hands wrestled him to the floor on his face, hands cuffed behind his back. "I am arresting you for breaking and entering and attempted burglary. Come quietly or you'll be sorry."

"But ... How...?" Brainlack gasped.

"We have our ways," said the police sergeant. "It will ensure that you miscreants are always caught and put away."

Once the criminal had been taken away, Jenny Bott and her son sidled out of the kitchen slowly, astounded that this ... this charade-like action had taken place in their house, almost before their eyes.

"We don't even know that person," Jenny exclaimed with a horrified gasp. "How did you know he was going to be here?"

"We have our sources, Madam, that we couldn't possibly reveal to you," the sergeant replied to her. "To get the information that we need to help solve crimes and take criminals off the streets, our informants must remain unidentified.

"Have you checked to see that nothing is missing?" he went on after a moment or two. "He didn't get the chance to do anything much, but you never know with these leeches."

"Everything that was worth anything is now in a secure location at our bank," Toby Bott assured the policeman. "We don't have much, but what we do have is now under secure lock and key."

<hr>

"What on earth was that fool trying to prove?" Boss Man spat out when he had heard the news of Brainlack's arrest following his attempted break-in in Richmond. "Trying to prove we are easy meat?"

"Trying to prove he can do anything you ask of him, more like," Gangman replied, a self-satisfied smirk almost gracing his face. "Thanks to him, the folks living in that house will shift everything of value into safe keeping.

"In the meantime," he went on eventually, "I have several easy pickings in mind that you might like. First, there's…"

His voice faded away as he shared the details of several more much easier targets with the Boss Man that removed the stones temporarily from his mind – for the time being.

Chapter 14

"Hal?" Abigail said quietly to her husband as she was feeding Georgie in the hospital. "You're very quiet today."

"Not really," he replied. "You're feeding yon little man and that needs a bit of quiet, doesn't it? Just thinking about Little James that I never saw."

"Me neither," she pointed out. "Exquisite pain saw to that."

"When shall we have his … funeral?" she went on slowly, finding it hard to restrain the tears that wanted to flow.

"We don't have to register his death officially," Hal stated as he normally would.

"Why not?" she queried sharply. "He was a living human being!"

"But technically, he wasn't, because he was stillborn. In other words, he wasn't alive when he came out of your body," he went on to explain gently, causing his wife to descend into heart felt sobs. Not sure if it was the right thing to do, he slid his arm around her shoulders and drew her heaving body to his gently.

"To have him buried properly, we need to acquire a written certificate that he wasn't born alive, signed by one of the medics," Hal added further. "I don't think it would be a good idea to take him back to the North Riding either."

"But…" she complained lamely.

"Think back to Poppy's Nanny Nell's funeral and burial," he suggested. "Not allowed to be taken out of the country, and she had lived here full time for a year or two."

He paused for a while, Abigail's head resting close to his heart, before suggesting they might perhaps purchase a small burial plot near to Nanny Nell, and to do the necessaries as soon as possible.

"Ross Senior would be the one to ask about this one," Hal finished, kissing little Georgie's head as he brought up a dose of wind and a mite of undigested milk onto his mother's cardigan. This brought a slight smile to both faces. "I need to find out also when we can have you home, both to Ross's place and then properly to Yorkshire."

"Where's Grace?" Abigail asked.

"In the waiting area with Poppy," Hal responded. "Bring her in to meet her new brother?"

Once his wife had agreed and taken her new baby from his crib, Hal left the room to retrieve his daughter. She had always been excited in a controlled way when there was something or someone new to see or meet. As soon as she stepped through the swing door into the ward, on seeing her mother holding her new baby, she stopped, with tears beginning to roll down her cheeks.

She turned to her dad and, sliding her arms around his waist, she drew herself to him and began to weep quietly. He held her close to try to stem the tears.

"I'm sorry it's not a sister, Gracie, but this is your little brother, Georgie," Hal said quietly. "Would you like to say hello to him?"

Releasing her father, she turned, dried her eyes on her handkerchief and blew her nose loudly, causing her dad to burst out laughing and her brother to start whimpering slightly.

She ambled across to where her mother was sitting in an easy chair next to the bed, her baby dressed in swaddling clothes, now sitting on her lap. Abigail held out her free arm for Grace to catch hold, to be drawn towards Georgie. Burying her face in his shawl, Grace sighed deeply.

"Not the sister I would have preferred, but I will love my brother Georgie nonetheless," she uttered decidedly, drawing a guffaw from Hal and giggles from Poppy and Abigail.

"You decided to do what?" Hal gasped, unable to understand or even accept what his wife was saying to him.

"It's the only sensible thing to do in our present circumstance," she started to explain in as reasonable and acceptable a manner as possible. "We all need to recover from what's happened recently and relax."

"Relax? How do you rationalise that one?" he reacted, seeking a plausible explanation to her outrageous suggestion. "We are not rich, and as such we need to earn money to … exist, don't you know."

"If we live here for the next six months, then surely we – you or I – can raise the wherewithal to live," Abigail said, trying to lay before her husband a sensible reason why they should remain … in Nice. "I have just had the most trying experience recently – as you know – and now I need time and space to recover, along with our little boy."

"Then we have to find somewhere to live," Hal asserted quickly. "It won't be cheap, and—"

"There is an ocean-facing apartment for sale or rent next door to me," Ross butted in as he re-entered the living room from the kitchen.

"Cost might be an issue," Hal replied.

"At no cost to you, Hal," Ross added with a smile and a nod.

"Because—?" Hal went on trying to finish his previous sentence.

"I own it," Ross continued, "and it's fully furnished and ready to move in."

"But we can't…" Hal flustered.

"Done deal, Old Chap, and no more to say about it," Ross finished, not allowing him to complete his weak objection. "You have done a lot for Poppy and now it's time for me to reciprocate."

"Then thank you so much," Abigail butted in sharply, throwing her arms about his neck in gratitude. "We will, of course, during the next six months be organising Poppy's return to book the launch and re-sale of her soon-to-be two titles *Faithfully Yours* and *And Now?*. Paris first followed by New York with London much later."

"Reasons being?" Hal asked lamely because his wife rarely involved him in the planning; only organising transport, accommodation and financial outlay – the less important aspects of the events, according to her.

"Certain 'difficulties' on and around Northern Europe, I had heard," she threw from the top of her head casually that she wouldn't be able to enlighten upon. "Ross knows more about that than I do, I would imagine."

"There has been political instability in the Balkans – Bosnia, Serbia and Herzegovina in particular – for some time," Ross began his general explanation. "This has threatened to destroy the agreements of a variety of alliances that have existed for many years – the Ottoman Empire, Russia and others to name but a few."

"I know nothing about any of this," Hal admitted, much

to Abigail's surprise. "Probably because we do not live here and because I have been otherwise engaged."

"It's quite likely to blow over because nobody in their right mind would wish to have a serious flare up that could end in conflict," Ross mused with a shrug. "Anyway, we'll sort out documentation for next door's occupation within the next day or two, and then you can move in lock, stock and barrel. It'll be good to have you all as our valued neighbours."

<hr>

"Daddy?" Grace began one of her deep questions that had Hal wondering what might be coming next.

"Yes, my beauty, what world-changing question do I need to think about now?" he responded seemingly flippantly, that his daughter always ignored.

"I heard Grandpa Ross talking about something that I didn't understand," she asked rather innocently.

"He talks about quite a few things that *I* don't understand," Hal assured her without lifting his face from his plans for their next adventure.

"That's probably because you rarely lift your head up to look at the person talking to you," Grace advised him, trying to look him in the eye, to the barely concealed amusement of her mother.

Putting down his quill ink pen, he lifted his face, with an apology to his child, and gave her his total attention.

"As I was saying," she went on gathering the attention of all the adults in the room, "I didn't understand what Grandpa Ross meant when he said something about a lock, a block and a barrel. Could you explain, please?"

Hal smiled and hesitated briefly while collecting his thoughts.

"It's a saying that goes back to the times soldiers were armed with firearms that were used for firing bullets that were meant to harm or kill their enemies. They were made up of three main parts – a *lock* which when released would send the bullet down a long metal tube called a *barrel* out to the target the soldier was aiming at. The wooden part of the firearm – called the *stock* – allowed the soldier to rest it against his shoulder to make it easier to aim and fire once he had pressed the trigger," he explained, pausing for a moment to gather his thoughts.

"The three parts – the lock, the stock and the barrel – had to be together to allow the firearm to work. Hence when people heard the saying 'lock, stock and barrel' they knew that everything was together."

"So," Grace butted in slowly, "if you were to tell me to gather *all* my toys together so we could go to our new apartment next door, I might ask 'lock, stock and barrel?' Would you understand what I was saying?"

Most of the adults in the room laughed at Grace's understanding even though she had never seen nor heard of a musket before.

"Absolutely lock, stock and barrel!" Hal guffawed. "Clever girl. So, I don't even need to mention it now."

Chapter 15

"It looks like we've done well locking away that idiot we brought in the other day," Sergeant Smith said to his superior officer, Inspector Shaw.

"I would still prefer to have my hands on his boss though," Inspector Shaw returned. "Then we could have taken down a whole gang of reprobates. We still need to keep tabs on our informer because it's through people like him we can make progress putting those toe-rags away."

"We need to keep our eyes on family and associates of Jonas Jamieson as well," the sergeant added. "He's no longer with us, but links always live on. There are still family ties that I believe we need to remember."

"Mother and son both live in the house in Richmond they inherited from him, though how he was able to afford to acquire it is still open to conjecture," the inspector pointed out. "At the moment his stepson drives a rather high-end taxi and gives us no cause to believe he is involved in nefarious activities. We still need to keep an eye open though."

"It was their house, of course, where we felt Brainlack's collar the other day," the sergeant went on. "Although it seems like it was nothing of *their* doing, I'm still not sure about that one."

~

"How did the police work out that that reprobate was about to break into our home?" Toby asked his mother a few days after the police had collared the intruder. "I certainly didn't alert them, because I didn't know it was about to happen."

"You know as much as me," she replied, trying hard to come to terms with the problem. "I wonder if it could have been anything to do with the diamond that now resides in the bank vault."

"Thinking back, the day before he was killed, Jonas warned me that he had something to give to you that he had wanted to do for some time," Toby said thoughtfully as a puzzled frown began to descend. "I wonder if the stone was the engagement 'ring' he had talked about on a number of occasions?"

Immediately Jenny burst into tears, her loss very palpable, although that depth of feeling was not shared publicly by her son. Jonas was the only father figure he had known, but it wasn't for long and emotionally it didn't affect him deeply, although he knew he would be eternally grateful for building secure foundations beneath him. They were the human building blocks that would allow his standards to grow and flourish.

After the birth of her son, her plans for a comfortable life had disappeared in a flash. She had planned that she would bring him up reasonably comfortably, but then she had to revisit and change those plans significantly. She was glad that her son had some sorts of standards to look up to, but not the ones she had envisaged, not in the early days anyway.

Living as roughly throughout her son's early years had been unconscionably difficult – squalidly unacceptable but necessary to say the least. She had felt that things would necessarily change when her son had been born, because of who his sire was. Things were unfortunately taken out of her hands.

"You never did tell me who my father was," Toby uttered once his mother's sobbing had settled. "But then probably you might not know because of your way of life."

"Don't you believe it, young man!" Jenny's temper flared at her son's dismissal. "I *do* know who your father was and always have. So don't you dare cast aspersions on my moral standards."

Shocked to hear his mother's outburst, yet wanting to know urgently the man that gave him life, he said, "And he was?"

"He was the grandfather of the young lady to whom you gave a taxi ride the other day," she burst forth. "Poppy Spence, the author."

"That gives me no clue at all," he scoffed, not sure where this was leading him – or her for that matter.

"He was called Joss McIntyre, and he owned Boulders Wood Farm, not that far away from here," she stated blandly. "A very wealthy landowner."

"Boulders Wood…?" he gasped, almost not believing what he had just been told. "I was there a few days ago! Why—?"

"He would never have been able to either let you know you were related, nor would he have admitted how you were conceived," she stated boldly.

Stopped in his tracks by her surprising explanation, his face dropped, and a deep non-understanding frown began to grow. Intrigued but not willing to take their conversation any further, they gravitated towards the kitchen to magic up a mug of tea and a piece of home-made cake which he was not aware his mother was able to bake.

"I'm not sure I really want to follow that route, Ross," Joseph pointed out firmly to his brother. "Too much effort, too much outlay, not enough return."

"Joe Smeddley, t'other side of Middlesbrough has just started a similar project," Ross replied. "I grant you he is having to redesign and redirect some of his reserves, but it sounds quite interesting."

"Not interesting enough for Boulders Wood, I have to say," his brother went on, a firm shaking of the head accompanying his doubts. "Just tell me, where can we raise enough capital and what can we redirect to be able to afford what you are suggesting?"

"There is undoubtedly a possible outlet for my suggestion," Ross insisted. "I was talking to the town's mayor the other day, and he suggested we might be interested in setting up some sort of an attraction to bring visitors into our area. Ours is the only place with enough space to do such like. Here's the thing. They would be prepared to give us a reasonable grant to help the funding."

A stark silence fell as Joseph drank his large mug of tea slowly, almost forcing his brother to halt *his* offensive. Once he had finished, he looked up at Ross and said, "OK then. Give me one idea that you feel might – I said *might* don't forget – be put in place with the least outlay, that might prove to be lucrative."

Looking at his brother's almost intractable face, a slight smile developed in Ross's eyes as he decided where to begin.

"We have a strong link with an excellent cake shop on the High Street in town," Ross started.

"Cake shop? In town…?" Joseph replied non-too sure of where this was taking him. "I don't—"

"Do you remember a couple of wonderful bakers called

Mary and Mary-Jane?" Ross said quietly, realising his brother's sense of humour either didn't stretch to meet his, or didn't exist at all.

"Of course I do!" Joseph complained, a little embarrassed that he hadn't appreciated his brother's reference ... or his humour. "So what?"

"Places where they sell 'home baked' goodies and allow people to sit at a table and partake also of a cup of tea or coffee are becoming very popular," Ross explained, not expecting his brother to grasp the relevance or importance. "It's called a 'café' and they are gaining in popularity nowadays."

Joseph remained quiet, unsure of what he might be letting himself in for should he agree tentatively.

"Our mentor and supplier of delicious stock would be, of course, Mary and Mary-Jane," Ross went on.

"Mentor?" his brother asked after a short while of thought, obvious by the descent of his 'serious' brow.

"As we have neither the inkling nor the time to learn and prepare, I have asked Mary and Mary-Jane if they might give us a hand in the areas we know nothing about," Ross threw in quickly. "In other words ... everything. Martha has said she would be happy to learn and take part should she be needed.

"Just one last thing to consider before you say either yay or nay," Ross continued, to add a bit more confusion onto Joseph's shoulders. "If you remember, we have a large space above and next to the milking parlour that, upon conversion, could become our 'café' where customers would be able to look down through the adjoining windows onto the cows being milked."

"I am totally confused now!" Joseph gasped, wiping his sweaty brow. "Perhaps you might like to give it some further thought and bring me a ... what do they call it? ... proposition, and then—?"

"It's already done, Bro," Ross replied with a satisfied grin. "I'll write it out and we can discuss matters in a day or two.

"Just one final thing," Ross added as his brother sat down finally with another mug of tea. "I should like you to bear in mind that we have two workers' cottages available for conversion…"

"Conversion into what?" Joseph gasped again. "Palaces?"

"Almost," Ross guffawed. "Into holiday cottages that people would pay a princely sum to be able to spend a week's holiday in the countryside. Motorcars are becoming more and more popular these days, allowing ordinary town people to visit our countryside. Right. I'm off. Work to do."

He strode out of the living room into the open, fresh air, ready to restart his work of the day, a happy grin to his stubbly face; thoughts of his brother's confused visage jostling about in his mind.

CHAPTER 16

"Daddy?" Grace asked slowly over tea in their 'new' apartment overlooking the Mediterranean. "Do you remember when our Queen died?"

"Yes, my lovely, I believe I do," Hal responded eagerly to his little girl's request. He loved requests like this from her as it showed how smart and eager to learn she was. "It was Tuesday 22nd January 1901. Why do you ask?"

"I know he was sixty years old when his mother died and he became King Edward VII," she went on. "But here's the thing … he was called Albert Edward after his father, Prince Albert, wasn't he? So why wasn't he crowned King Albert Edward?"

"He chose it himself," Hal replied quite simply. "His mother – Victoria – had wanted him to be called King Albert Edward, but he didn't want to undervalue the name of his father whom he felt should have stood alone. He felt he should have been called King Albert."

Grace fell quiet for a short while taking in all she had been told, as she usually did when her father had shared interesting information with her.

"Here's another interesting thing," Hal went on, getting

103

into his stride. "His coronation had been arranged for 26th June 1901 but had to be put off because, two days before, he had developed appendicitis. That wasn't a condition that was usually subject to surgery because it was very dangerous, and he could have died."

"Well, he's still alive, isn't he?" Grace noted knowledgeably. "So, why…?"

"The appendix was an organ in his belly that had grown what they called an 'abscess'," he explained. "The surgeon cut through his belly and removed a pint of pus, curing him of his appendicitis."

"Eugh!" Grace groaned, pulling an ugly face. "I didn't know you could have a cat in your stomach!"

"In this case, pus is a nasty infectious fluid," Hal explained with a hearty guffaw. "He recovered and was crowned King Edward VII in Westminster Abbey on 9th August 1901, by the Archbishop of Canterbury, Frederick Temple."

"I do like this apartment," Grace said, changing the subject quickly. "The views are lovely."

"One thing about King Edward VII that most people don't know?" he finished, drawing her attention away from the view. "He spent his annual summer holiday in Southwestern France in Biarritz, about five hundred miles away from here, whereas before he was crowned, his holidays had always been here on the French Riviera."

"So, you like the apartment, Gracie?" her mother asked, flitting away from Hal's boring conversation.

"I love it because I like to spend time—" she began with a smile.

"On your own or … with your dad," Abigail interrupted quietly. "Yes, we know."

"And with you, Mammy," Grace jumped in quickly as she

shuffled over to put her arms around her mother.

A loud banging on the outside door startled them all but drew Hal to its noise. Both mother and daughter could hear voices beginning to raise somewhat in anger until Hal backed into the living room, keeping a Frenchman at bay with his more than ample hands. The Frenchman's broken English was brushed aside by Hal's impeccable French, much to the Frenchman's surprise, which fortunately settled his anger as he turned and retreated out from the apartment the way he came in.

Mother and daughter looked at each other, perplexed at what they had just witnessed.

"I didn't know you could speak French, Hal," Abigail puzzled, surprised at what she had just witnessed.

"Never had to use it before," he responded calmly.

"Then … why?" she threw back at him.

"It turns out that he thought we were in his apartment," Hal explained. "It wasn't until I told him that you were related to King Edward VII that he backed down, apologised and beat a hasty retreat."

Mother and daughter looked at each other again and burst into hearty laughter.

"What?" Hal responded, an almost surprised look growing in his face.

"Lilly Victoria? Martha?" George whispered, noticing his sisters sitting either side of his hospital bed as his eyes opened slowly. "Where am I and why are *you* here?"

Turning to face their brother, they both grinned happily, relieved that he had finally awoken.

"Remember nothing from the last four days, Our George?"

Martha asked as she stroked his hand; something that she rarely did, and he knew it.

"It must have meant something rather … serious, or you wouldn't be stroking my hand now," he noticed and commented. "Am I about to … die?"

"It was touch and go for quite some time," Lilly Victoria explained seriously. "Dr Twist thought it would be a good idea for us to be here in case…"

"In case I didn't make it?" George queried as he shuffled into a sitting position. "I remember nothing about the last four days. Absolutely … nothing. What has been wrong with me, and why am I here?"

"You passed out and we thought at one stage that you had … gone," Martha said in a low voice, a look of disquiet resting in her eyes.

"Fortunately, Dr Twist knew you weren't but felt that this was the best place for you," Lilly Victoria added.

"I have a very profound feeling you are about to put me straight, but … is Annabel … all right?" George asked, not confident he was about to receive the answer he required,

"I don't know how to tell you this but—" Lilly Victoria started quietly.

"She's gone, George, along wi' t'nipper she was carrying," Martha butted in quickly, straightforward as ever. "Buried a few days ago and … you were there."

"Not what I had hoped for, but I had a deep feeling there was something … not right," he replied, the tears already coursing down his craggy cheeks. "Alone again, eh?"

"Two things, Brother," Martha insisted non-too-softly. "You still have four sisters that love you, and of course a dear little girl who needs you desperately. She's gone through at least as much as you, losing her mother whom she never

met, and her twin in such a stark situation. She needs you …
unconditionally."

"How long do I have to stay here?" he asked after a few
minutes of silent consideration. He hadn't given his daughter
too much thought, having cast his mind selfishly towards his
own problems. Perhaps he needed to draw away from his own
self-guided thoughts to reinvest in her present and future. He
knew his sisters and their partners would always be there, but
… Maisie? "Where *is* my daughter?"

"You need to stay here until you feel well enough to re-start
your life, which does, of course, include her," Lilly Victoria
insisted, to the nod of agreement from her sister Martha. "She
has been with us at Boulders Wood for some time now, in
default of having her own mother's attention to enjoy."

"Dr Twist will advise you on when to go back to your
normal life," Martha pointed out. "He's just shouldering his
way through the ward's doors now."

"George? How are you feeling?" the doctor asked with a
smile. "Feel like going home?"

C H A P T E R 1 7

"At least £2,600," Toby said to his mother over their luscious evening meal of roast pork, crackling, stuffing, mashed potatoes and sprouts.

"It certainly did not!" she huffed in return.

"Are we talking at cross purposes here?" he asked more than a little puzzled by her response. "What—?"

"The cost?" she responded, even more puzzled. "The meal? It can't have been the cost of the meal."

"No, but it could be what we are able to sell this house for," he explained with a relieved grin. "I called in at the broker's – what they call 'estate agents' – after I saw an article in the Country Life Magazine about the value of houses these days."

"Magazine? You?" she queried, unsure of where this conversation was leading.

"Do you remember our conversation of a little while ago?" Toby reminded her. "Selling up and perhaps taking off to somewhere … warmer? I saw the advertisement for estate agents Walton and Lee, so I nipped in for some information."

"Oh," she shrugged. "I see. And?"

"In default of having an official valuation, they gave me

an approximate amount we might achieve were we to sell," he told her.

"Which is?" she responded after his pause.

"The chap said probably £2,666," Toby said quietly. "Plus their costs."

"Is that a lot of money?" she asked, not understanding much about values and such like, as she had never owned property before this house was gifted to her by Jonas Jamieson.

"Enough, I should imagine, to allow us to live where we would like," he stated with a sweep of his arm. "Even – dare I say it? – the South of France."

"Could this be anything to do with that author woman you have become friendly with recently?" Jenny asked, a sly little smile gracing her lips.

"Poppy Spence?" he responded slowly. "And why not, if it is?

"All I want is to live somewhere with a better climate than here, and where we can escape from the violent ne'er-do-wells that plague the place," he added as he pushed away his almost empty dinner plate. "Somewhere I can do my job of earning a living and looking after my mother in peace and tranquillity."

"Aww!" Jenny eulogised, tears gathering in her eye corners. "Then let's do it."

That was not what he expected from his uncomprehending mother. He had always been used to seeing her fall into line with the men in her life. What could he expect from her from now on? He picked at his pudding, unsure where this might lead them. Was this the right time to have this conversation?

"Perhaps we need to pursue what we should do when we have a little more solid information at our fingertips?" he added, hoping to end the discussion that was beginning to add weight to his shoulders.

Joseph stood in the courtyard of their farm, hands resting on hips, a seemingly vacant look on his face as he stared at the unused conglomeration of stone-built but empty barns surrounding his glazed expression and motionless body.

"Just what *I* was thinking," Ross's deep voice jolted him from his dreamy world back to reality.

"Didn't either see or hear you approaching," his brother replied as he turned quickly to face the newcomer. "And you mean…?"

"The three empty barns are adjacent and attached to our milking parlour," Ross explained. "Within the one closest to it, a café could be created, with a large glass window overlooking where our cows are milked."

"And why would that be important?" Joseph asked pointedly.

"Customers might wish to watch while having a drink and something to eat," Ross explained further. "On the ground floor there might be some sort of an outlet where the beautiful baking provided by Mary and Mary-Jane could be purchased and taken away. A bit like having their High Street bakery in the … countryside."

"Glad to catch you two together in one place at last," a broad Yorkshire voice attacked the brothers from behind. It was their gamekeeper, Jim Smallshore, causing the brothers to turn sharply. "I hear what you are saying about a café and sales outlet. An excellent idea that has been done by one or two much smaller farms in the East Riding."

Ross grinned and pointed his outstretched right index finger at Jim, obviously grateful for the support he needed.

"Now here's another idea," Jim went on. "Rabbits are—"

"A darned nuisance, we know," Joseph agreed with a sage nod. "We know also that you are in the process of—"

"Hatching a plan to make a significant business out on 'em," Jim butted in.

"How come?" Ross asked, intrigued at what he was hearing. "Tell me more, Jim."

"I know of quite a few farmers that are sharing and selling 'em to t'public as a popular – and tasty – meat source, as they've allus bin," Jim explained.

"If I know you, Jim Smallshore, you will have gone a few steps further," Ross replied eagerly. "By making it easier to catch and sell 'em?"

"Here's the thing," Jim began. "Ifn we build artificial warrens, allowing rabbits to occupy and breed in 'em, we can guarantee an unstoppable source of fresh rabbit meat for the public to buy. We already know of a variety of suppliers that are desperate to increase their stocks.

"Come with me and I'll show you what I mean," Jim offered, leading the brothers off towards the woods close by.

～

"Well now, that's something I did not expect!" Ross gasped as they turned the wooded corner at the forest end of the lake. Before their astounded eyes lay a series of low-rise mounds of grass-covered earth that would be manageable for the guardians looking after them.

"'Pillow mounds' is what you see before you," Jim explained roundly. "They are a series of tunnels and lairs that have been constructed to provide the rabbits with shelter, breeding space, and protection from the elements and predators."

"But how does it work?" Joseph queried.

"They serve as controlled environments where rabbit populations can be securely bred, sheltered and harvested," Jim replied confidently. "All we have to do is to allow nature to take its course, which lets us harvest and sell."

"What about your work with other animals, Jim," Joseph asked pointedly. "Doesn't it—?"

"Meks no difference at all," Jim responded sharply as they turned to leave. "This is mi 'obby. Joseph. I've nowt else to do wi' mi time, and I enjoy doin' it. And … I 'ave no need for payment, if that's what you're concerned about. I'll si thi later. I'm off to see to mi stock as we're 'ere. All mi other work's bin done."

"I wasn't—" Joseph tried to defend himself as Jim disappeared into the trees.

"Well done, Brother," Ross chided Joseph for casting some sort of aspersion in their gamekeeper's direction. "Don't forget that we are very lucky to have Jim here, doing stuff he has cleverly thought through. You'll have to find ways to reward – financially – his efforts to bring fresh finance into Boulders Wood. Now we need to do *our* homework as far as viability of the product is concerned, and then we can leave it to Jim to run it through."

CHAPTER 18

"Will I ever go to school here, Daddy?" Grace asked as she put down her writing quill and picked up her favourite reader.

"Excellent," he replied, noticing her choice of book. "*Heidi* by Johanna Spyri? I'm glad you enjoy your books. This is one of the reasons why you won't be drafted into any French schools. Your witing is very good along with your arithmetic and you are English which gives you a very good start with reading. Other books?"

"I have *Anne of Green Gables* by L. M. Montgomery, *The Call of the Wild* by Jack London, and *The Jungle Book* by Rudyard Kipling in my bag," she offered. "So, I hope we won't be staying here too long otherwise I will need to buy some more."

She gave her father one of her withering looks which told him her growing library of books needed to carry on expanding to maintain her literary development.

"Not sure whether we will be able to buy any books for you written in English, because this is—" Hal returned with a naughty grin.

"France, I know," Grace butted in. "This is one of the

reasons I will be happy to be at home ... along with the food."

"Not happy with what's put on the table?" Hal queried. "Not sure how to cure that without moving back to England—"

"Lock, stock and barrel!" Grace threw into the conversation with a wicked giggle.

"It won't be too much longer, my sweetie," Abigail promised as she sidled onto the balcony with Little Georgie in her arms.

"But...?" Hal queried with a puzzled frown. "I thought you wanted..."

"Georgie and I are feeling much better," Abigail pronounced, assuring her family of her improvement and the progress of their surviving son. "So, just another week or two in Nice's lovely climate should suffice. "Fancy a little stroll along the front in the sunshine, Gracie?

"We need to be planning Poppy's next event, too," she reminded her husband. "One of three choices really, I think."

"*Three* choices?" Hal said with some degree of uncertainty.

"Paris, London, New York," she responded, nodding vigorously, sure of those choices.

"Just one or two problems around timing for each of those locations," Hal pointed out. "Don't forget that I have undertaken a certain amount of detailed planning with varying degrees of success. Because of certain ... climatic or citizen difficulties, we will have to time our visits accurately."

"Difficulties?" Abigail questioned as they walked along the Promenade des Anglais in the healing sunshine. "How do you mean?"

"There have tended to be ... problems with winter floods in Paris, limiting the times visits can be made to the city; river rising more rapidly than at any other time from the sewer system, for example," Hal began to explain. "In some cases, the river rose twenty feet above its normal level."

"Then we don't go in winter?" Abigail reasoned. "Sound sense?"

"Yes, but not guaranteed," he responded with a shake of the head. "The other, much more dangerous situation revolves around certain alliances forged between a variety of nations in Europe in the run up to the turn of the century in 1900. Europe now is very much less stable … and safe than at any other time."

"This makes me think that not only should we leave Paris alone as a book launch venue because of the physical dangers, but also because of the wider aggravations between countries," Abigail insisted, a look of horror invading her face. "Does this mean, then, that we need to vacate this area as soon as necessary?"

"Indeed, but not through any desperate hurry," Hal agreed. "As you said before, within the next week or two, perhaps."

Grace sat in the corner of the veranda, her mind buried in the Heidi text she was engrossed in, oblivious to the troubles and difficulties her parents wrestled with reasonably quietly but pragmatically.

~

"What is it you find so … attractive here?" Sarah asked Poppy over an afternoon tea and cakes outside a local café. "I mean, is it somewhere you might live forever?"

"I love this area of the world as do many others like Queen Victoria who spent a lot of summertime round here. Her son, Prince Edward, did the same before he became king. Funnily enough, when he did become king, he ceased taking his holidays here and started somewhere new – Biarritz at the other side of the country," Poppy replied, gazing out to sea. This took her mind back to the first time she stayed by the North Sea at Scarborough with her friends when she was twelve. Same sort of feeling, although the temperature then was somewhat lower than in Nice. "Not sure where I'll be when I am Grandpa's age, though."

"You'll be exactly as you are now, I am sure," Rosie butted in with a smile. "I think *I've* found my forever place. How about you, Sister?"

"Can't say," Sarah reacted after a pause that emphasised her words. "Maybe; maybe not. I'm still trying to take it all in. Situation where I'm still absorbing the effect of finding my family is having on me. Confused and bemused, really. Ask me the same question in a year's time, perhaps. Haven't got to know Father yet."

"He's a difficult one to understand," Rosie added profoundly. "Very deep, yet … simple to get on with."

"Can't help wishing he had been around when I was a child," Rosie returned after a moment's thought.

"I could say the same about you!" Sarah rejoined. "I was convinced there ought to have been much more to my life when I was six but—"

"I was told not," her twin finished off her sentence.

"This is the sort of thing I would have loved to have had as part of my life then," Sarah acknowledged with a deep sigh. "Nobody to play with in the Outback. No family even to talk to. So pleased I'm here, enjoying my life, and why I'm staying until the good Lord says otherwise."

"This is where you and I differ, both Rosie and Sarah," Poppy acknowledged "I had friends right from being seven years old – both female and male. Unfortunately, some of those very dear people are no longer with us, whom I miss very deeply."

Poppy suddenly closed up, eyes filling with earnest tears that she neither could nor wanted to staunch. Her friends Florence, Alice and Annabel all crept unashamedly into her mind from different memories that she often experienced; to as far back as her twelfth birthday anniversary on the east coast with them. Then there was … George Garside. How was *he* doing now?

"Daddy?" Maisie asked carefully quietly. "Will you be coming home with us today? Only…"

"Try to keep me away!" George responded, sliding his legs out of his hospital bed. As his bare feet touched the icy floor, he gasped, expecting to feel the warm if dishevelled rug he never moved from his easy chair in the living room at Garside Farm.

Feeling a little dizzy because of the time he had spent on his back, he leaned carefully on the small bedside cabinet to steady himself and to prevent another accident to which he seemed prone these days.

Sitting back on the edge of the bed, his mind wound its way towards the most recent disasters he had experienced – the loss of his two wives, two nippers, his parents and … the love of his life, Poppy Spence. How could he have let her escape from his life on so many occasions – the woman he was destined to have married … or lose?

Would he ever see her again?

CHAPTER 19

"Do you remember our conversation of a short while ago, Brother?" Ross tried to remind Joseph.

"And which one was that?" Joseph replied absent-mindedly while feeding the new sheep in the north field by the lake. "We have so many conversations that either interrupt my mid-morning break or fill my head with memories that disappear almost immediately."

"Your answer then would be 'No'?" Ross retorted, knowing full well he was wasting his time trying to remind him of anything important that might need a definite answer. "Café? Cows being milked? Extra income?"

"Oh," Joseph reacted slowly as if catching the whisper of a passing unimportant discussion. "Slipped my mind, I'm afraid."

"As does virtually everything that might have an effect on our managing income and finance in general," his brother burst out, barely able to contain his anger at his brother's seemingly lame dismissal of anything important Ross might raise. "You need to get a grip of yourself, Old Man, or this farm will suffer the fate of many others that have disappeared in the North of this country!"

"Hang on a bit!" Joseph complained as he dropped the animal feed bucket and turned to face his brother. "Does it not occur to you that I have a lot on my mind most of the time?"

"Too much for you to realise that you have someone close who does just as much as you do but who can take decisions that might just make a difference to the success of this farm?" Ross countered.

This stopped Joseph in his tracks, making him realise that his brother not only had a valid point but also that he might be trusted to take some of the burden from his brother's shoulders.

"What do you want me to say?" Joseph rejoined after a few minutes' silence.

"Just to listen and revisit what I had to say about developing our public offerings to bring in revenue to keep us in business," Ross advised. "I've spoken to Mary about setting up the café and supplying us initially with the wherewithal to bring success. She suggested also children's swings and roundabouts to help to draw in families. Remember also the bit about refurbishing those two almost derelict cottages to provide holiday lets?"

Joseph sat down on a nearby rock with a resigned bump, unsure how he was going to react to both having forgotten and how he had treated his brother. Seemingly with lack of respect and understanding.

"I think you should be the one to pursue all you have raised here, then," Joseph fielded quietly. "All you have to bear in mind is—"

"Cost and quality?" Ross countered with a resigned grin. "I know, Brother, I know. Am I allowed to get on with those two items, then?"

His brother nodded sagely not wishing to cause friction

with a brother that did more than anyone else to ensure that matters ran as smoothly as possible to ensure fewer problems for him.

Stopping what he was doing sharply and facing Ross quizzically, he said, "You've spoken with Mary about commodities for this … café?"

"I have," Ross answered as he turned to go.

"You haven't left Boulders Wood for more than a week, so how?" Joseph asked. "By shouting?"

Ross guffawed loudly at his brother's amusing naïvety. "Ever heard of a black machine called a 'telephone'?"

Then it was back to his work outside as the sky started to turn an ominously dark shade, and intermittent white flakes began to dot the air.

Although Joseph trusted his brother's instincts concerning his desires to make their business future-proof, he wasn't a lover of introducing what he called 'foreigners' into his home. Granted they wouldn't be in his actual domain, but they could be close enough to cause him concern.

As usual, Ross had taken everything in his stride, organising both the working staff for the conversion of the milking parlour annex and its planning, furnishing, and its financial implications. Mary had introduced Ross to an invaluable source of second-hand furniture – tables and chairs and cupboards – to minimise the costs, along with donating some of her spare – older – cutlery and crockery. She had also promised publicity for the café's opening and its initial running; for six months at any rate.

"How long is all this work going to take, Ross, for something we have no idea will succeed?" his wife, Martha, asked at breakfast a month or so into the project.

"Mary tells me it should take no longer than six months," he announced. "She's arranging for staff to run it on a daily basis for a few months with her in charge I hasten to add, and then it will be up to us."

"I would love to be involved," she added unexpectedly, causing her husband to stop his breakfast mid-chew. Although she was a lovely cook and baker, he had always felt she would perhaps be a little too shy and unassuming to be part of such a public show.

"But I thought—" he reacted with a puzzled frown and a shrug.

"That I wouldn't want to be involved?" she questioned. "You never asked."

***

"I have no choice," George responded to his four sisters who seemed to be ganging up on him when he finally reached home after his stay at the hospital's behest. "I have two flocks of sheep to see to, and a lot more to look towards on the farm!"

"You've no choice if you want to kill yourself," Lilly Victoria replied with disdain. "Ross and Joseph have been seeing to your flocks and—"

"And I'm grateful to them both," George butted in. "But they don't know what needs doing and when."

"They've been farming since before you were born," Martha retorted sharply. "So, your sheep have been well looked after, even to your stores of feed being replenished."

"My farm. My decision," he returned finally.

"Then don't come complaining to us when you realise you need help!" Charity warned. "I cannot believe your attitude towards those who have given their time and thought without having to be asked."

George fell backwards into his chair with a frustrated sigh. Was this another of his decisions that could be called into question – again?

"If you need help, oh awkward brother, for goodness' sake ask," Lilly Victoria suggested as she and Martha unsnecked the front door ready to return to their homes at Boulders Wood.

Charity nodded to her sister, Florence, quietly beckoning towards the kitchen door as they left the living room to prepare their midday meal, leaving their brother to his thoughts. His daughter, Maisie, was with her cousins at Boulders Wood where she always spent her days because of her father's usual work in the fields with his flocks.

The time George spent on his own always allowed him to revisit his baseline decisions and to review the sensible advice others had offered to him. Why couldn't he make the sorts of wise decisions that others almost always came up with? Where did these ideas come from that inevitably set him at odds with those close to him? Following the advice given freely without reference wasn't perhaps the proper thing to do, but possibly he would learn from it and become a better person because of it.

Probably his sheep wouldn't suffer if he remained in his chair to rest for a while…?

"Daddy! Daddy!" an insistent little voice poked through George's unconsciousness. "Are you … alive? Daddy, please don't be … dead!"

"It's all right my Little One," George replied through a yawn and a groan. "I'm here. I've only been asleep for a little while."

Maisie threw her arms about his neck as he drew her to him, the only one really close to him nowadays.

This was why he needed to change everything in his life.

She was the one person for whom a new view on his life was important, and for whom he had to change his thinking. She deserved his full attention at all times, which she had never received before.

For him a new day had just dawned.

123

CHAPTER 20

"New York should be our next adventure, I believe," Hal said definitively. "If we are to do anything."

"And the reason for that is?" Abigail replied, quizzing his logic.

"As we discussed very briefly a little while ago, Paris has gone through serious times lately – both physical and political," he returned, a serious look growing in his face.

"Is it basically what you brought up before?" his wife challenged him. "Nothing more difficult, I hope?"

"Floods that have not been caused by the River Seine overflowing its banks," he began in earnest according to Hal's nature. "The excess waters from the winter rains come up through the sewers leaving its glorious effluent everywhere.

"Unfortunately," he went on, after taking a breath, "Baron Haussmann's larger sewer tunnels that had been engineered in the late 1870s has worsened the destruction caused by the floods."

"But that's not been a year-round problem, has it?" Abigail asked, not sure where this discussion was heading. "The other difficulty you mentioned? Political?"

"Darkening days ahead have been forecast, I'm afraid," Hal

responded after a moment's thought. "During the late 1890s a variety of European nations signed mutual agreements, ostensibly to support each other in darker times. Tensions apparently have been brewing throughout Europe, particularly in the Balkans."

"Balkans? Where's that?" Abigail queried. "Never heard of that place before."

"Southeastern Europe," he explained. "Bosnia, Serbia, Herzegovina – thereabouts.

"Mark my words," he went on, a dour look draining his usually serious but happy face. "Nothing good will come of this … trouble, and politicians being politicians, conflict could erupt at any time."

"What about us in England?" Abigail wondered, a horrified air about her. "Will we become involved?"

"Who knows?" he retorted with a shrug. "Things like this have happened before. If we are not careful as a nation, it could turn into a world conflict involving many people."

"New York it is then," Abigail acknowledged. "Remembering our last foray into that city, I suppose we need to be wary of anything local that might happen. Remember the chap with the gun?"

"And I will never forget how you dealt with his demands!" he scoffed loudly. "I wonder if he woke up with a bit of a headache."

They both sniggered at the image of Abigail, stick in hand, standing close by while a police presence attended to an unconscious lout on the bookshop floor in a gathering pool of blood."

"Same bookshop?" Abigail suggested for their new visit.

"As we sold a heck of a lot of copies last time, I see no reason why not," Hal urged. "If it's all right with you – and

Poppy, of course – I'll arrange it for the summertime."

~

"Mother!" Toby called out as he returned from a busy day at work. "Mother, I'm home!"

Silence. Puzzled at the stillness of their house when she was usually waiting for him with a mug of her excellent tea on the living room's coffee table. Had she gone shopping for something he loved for his tea? He knew she wouldn't be visiting friends … she didn't have any.

He walked through into the third bedroom that they had converted to a smaller sitting room, concerned that she might either be asleep in Jonas Jamieson's favourite chair, or have fallen and was injured or unconscious.

The room was dark because of the closed heavy velvet curtains at the picture window. Stepping slowly and warily quietly across the room to switch on the desk side lights, he tried not to wake the human shape in her comfortable chair. He wanted to wake his mother gently and pleasantly without shock.

Once he had switched on the gentle light, he turned slowly to find his mother's head was tipped to one side, and her eyes were staringly open. Unexpectedly shocked at seeing her like this, he touched her cheek to find that she was cold and obviously had been dead for some time. Noticing the ligature marks across her throat, he suspected the worst.

~

"Not natural causes, I'm afraid Mr Bott," the police sergeant offered sternly. "And you say there was no sign of forced entry when you returned home from work?"

"None, Sergeant," Toby returned quietly sad, not understanding when, who or why anyone would want to harm his inoffensive mother. "I'll check more thoroughly, but I don't think anything's been taken."

"Then it looks like what the French call a 'crime passionnel' or crime of passion," the sergeant offered. "We too will do our best to move forward with this one, but I don't hold out much hope."

Slumping onto the settee once the police had left, taking his mother's body to the mortuary, sadly he started to reassess his place in this world. With no family that he knew of and the dangers hovering around his place in this house and town, thoughts began to wave him towards his ideas on leaving the country totally; the fresh start he had tried to persuade his mother to move towards. If only she'd listened!

He had his suspicions concerning her killer, but in default of any real evidence, there was nothing he could do to redress the imbalance. He loved his mother dearly but now had to move on … and away.

A heavy banging at the front door drove all thoughts about his future from his head. Wary about the source of the intrusion, he opened the door on its security chain to someone he didn.t recognise.

"Yes? Who are you?" Toby asked carefully.

"John Filbert from Walton and Lee, property brokers," the young man responded.

"Walton and…?" Toby puzzled initially, unsure of the caller's identity. "Of course! I remember. Please come in."

He slid the door chain from its fastening and beckoned the caller to enter, only to replace it when the chap was inside.

"Cup of tea?" Toby asked politely, realising immediately that there was nobody there to make it. He explained to his visitor the situation with his mother as they sat by the fire in the main living room.

"No tea for me, thank you," the newcomer said, sitting on the edge of an easy chair. "I don't like the stuff. Besides, I have other calls to make so I need to be brief.

"My boss has asked me to give you this," he went on after a moment of rummaging through his worn briefcase, to withdraw an official-looking envelope from its innards. "Please read it and perhaps give him a telephone call as soon as possible."

He jerked from the easy chair, aware of what he had to achieve before his return to the firm's offices in town, and, straightening his coat he marched to the front door. Stepping quickly onto its worn door stone, he disappeared around the corner of the house, leaving the door ajar. Rushing to ensure his safety inside, Toby locked the door and reattached its security chain.

Puzzled both by the young man's visit and more so by the envelope he had brought, he tore it open, unfolded its contents and read what had been printed simply on it.

Sitting down with a shocked bump, he read the paper twice more to make sure he hadn't imagined what it said.

"I don't believe it!" Toby gasped quietly. "£3,500? And there's someone willing to pay cash to be able to move in as soon as possible?"

Picking up the telephone from its black cradle, he dialled a number and waited.

"Hello?" a crackly voice answered. "Walton and Lee, property brokers. Mr Walton's secretary speaking. How may I help you?"

<hr>

"You do realise of course that to allow customers to sample your glorious café's tasty morsels and coffees, you will have to make sure as many people as possible will know you are here,"

Mary reminded Ross as she served him tea and a buttered scone in Mary's Pantry. "No Joseph today?"

"He's passed all responsibility over to me, I'm afraid," Ross replied with a guffaw. "And by letting customers know you mean?"

"Telling them, somehow, that we are open for visits?" Martha interrupted.

"I should think it might be better if I dealt with you, Martha," Mary suggested as she turned to Ross's wife. "Men are none too good with this sort of organisation."

"I can vouch for that," Mary's husband, Geoffrey, agreed, nodding vigorously.

"What do you think we should do to alert customers to our existence, then?" Ross asked, puzzled by all this new thinking.

"Advertisement in local newspapers," Martha suggested, "along with leaflets printed by a local printer to deliver to us at Boulders Wood."

"I've onny ever seen local newspapers at the market day taverns but I'm sure we can sort summat out," Ross offered, scratching his head.

"*Daily Gazette* in Middlesbrough, *Knaresborough Post*, *Ripon Gazette*, and *Redcar and Saltburn News*, to name but a few," Martha threw into the mix.

"*Whitby Gazette, York Herald*, and *Ripon Observer*," Geoffrey added with gusto. "I lived in all three places before I met and married my lovely Lady. They were very popular and were circulated widely in all those towns.

"The only printing company I know of is based in York," he went on after a pause to think. "That was – and is – *Yorkshire Printing Works*. Easy to get to see in central York not that far from the Minster. We could find it easily I should think."

CHAPTER 21

Never having been to Yorkshire's East Coast at Scarborough or Bridlington before, Toby stood in awe as he left the railway station, suitcase in hand, to gaze at the sun glistening in the clear blue sky above him. The street just five steps in front of him was busy – even busier than he had ever seen any of the streets he had travelled along in his relatively short life in Yorkshire's North Riding.

Several taxis he could see plying their trade, but none even close to his own luxury vehicle. However, he would have to engage one to take him to the hotel where he had reserved a room for a month.

Mission accomplished, he sank into the comfortable rear seat, ready to start a new adventure. More than a little concerned that his taxi driver seemed to be driving on a different side of the road from him, he maintained his silence until he realised that every vehicle on this road – The Avenue de la Victoire – was doing the same.

This was something he would have to get used to pronto! Turning right onto the Promenade des Anglais, Toby gasped in awe at the sight of the sheet of calm, deep blue water that leaped into his eyes as the taxi slowed outside the Hotel West

End that was to be his home for at least the next few weeks, by the Mediterranean Sea on the French Riviera in Nice.

He had never seen such a sight at any time in his taxi-driving life! So, this was the seaside resort that Poppy Spence had told him about! How could she, a mere writer of stories, afford to live in a place such as this?

'Nees is nice,' he thought to himself with a silent snigger. He would have to get used to the view of the Mediterranean's 'Baie des Anges – The Bay of the Angels – as his hotel boasted this glorious view from most of its rooms.

～

"I don't believe it!" a female voice accosted Toby from behind as he sat on a seat overlooking the Mediterranean Sea. Surprised, he turned sharply to see a welcome beautiful face. "Toby Bott! No taxi?"

"Poppy Spence?" he responded, a surprised frown taking over his face as he stood up sharply. "I know you spend a lot of time hereabouts, but … now?"

"Preparing for my next book event – probably in North America – but the best place to stay in between events is here with my grandpa and my twin aunts," she explained. "Yet, I never expected to see you here. How—?"

"My mother was attacked and died in our house while I was at work," he replied. "So, I sold up and decided to give this place a try … following on from our conversation the last time I gave you a lift."

"Good choice," she agreed with a cheery smile. "Permanent stay?"

"Don't know," he responded. "I suppose it all depends on whether I can afford to buy a place and find something to do with my time, like working."

"Where are you staying? Anywhere ... Nice?" she asked with a grin.

He burst into a fit of giggles at her clever use of the word. "Good to see why you sell your stories ... You *do sell* your stories, I assume," he added with a strained look, but knowing well what she did. "I'm staying at the Hotel West End."

"Indeed, yes," she countered. "A lot of people have enjoyed my first effort, as you know, and *that* I am very pleased about. Don't know about the next one though. Posh hotel, I believe, where I've never stayed before.

"You must come around to visit us until you find your feet," Poppy added as she made to leave, offering him her business card with name, address and telephone number. "Lots of people here, but it can be lonely if you don't know anyone. I'd love you to meet Grandpa ... and Rosie and Sarah."

"Rosie and...?" he puzzled, not recognising the names.

"My twin aunts, but that's another story," Poppy sniggered at the strange look on his face as she turned to leave. "I'll telephone you next week!" she called just before she carried on back to her grandpa's apartment further down the Promenade des Anglais.

How strange and coincidental that he should meet someone he already knew on the first day of his new life in a new country. He had a strong feeling that he was about to put his old life behind him and look forward to whatever this new one was about to throw in his direction.

He supposed that he would need to look for somewhere decent to live, bearing in mind that he might not be able to afford his present accommodation forever.

⁓

"George?" sister Florence said, surprised to see her brother already downstairs fully dressed and sitting in his favourite easy chair. "Are you all right? Did you not sleep very well last night?"

"Never better … well, better than I was yesterday," he announced with a cheery smile. "Decided to take the advice given to me by my four sisters. Having thought seriously about my situation, I owe it to everyone to do what I need to do to improve my health, for as long as it takes."

"Oh dear!" Florence gasped in mock surprise, bearing in mind the George she knew *never* listened to anyone else. "I nearly fainted there!"

"Cheek," he responded with an understanding smile. "I will therefore allow you to cook me a poached egg on toast for my breakfast."

"Not sure that I can," she replied playfully. "But I'll give it a try."

Once she had disappeared into the kitchen to prepare their first meal of the day, his mind turned towards Poppy, as it often had. He still couldn't get a handle on not knowing where she was, but even when he was able to see her in the flesh, he didn't know how to deal with her presence. He had spent so much physical time causing problems … time that should have resulted in their union. Would he ever accept their precarious position for the rest of his life?

"Daddy!" Maisie's voice brought him back to life, along with her little body landing on his lap.

"Oof!" he gasped with a chuckle. "You *are* getting heavier, my little peach. You'll be squashing me flat before long, I'm sure.

"I thought you usually stayed with your cousins during the day," he continued after a moment or two cuddling his daughter which they hadn't done for some time.

"Uncle Ross and Auntie Martha thought it would do us both good if we were together today for a while," Maisie explained.

"Good thinking," he answered. "It might be a good idea for us to do this every day while I am recuperating, don't you think?"

"Re … coo … per …ating?" Maisie tried to copy his word. "What is that?"

"Recuperating means … getting better," he explained. "And I think you'll make that happen quicker, my lovely."

At this point the kitchen door bounced open as Florence brought a tray of food in for them all, to the looks of delight on each face.

George's real recuperation had begun its course.

Abigail's life had its high-ups and by stark contrast its very low downs. She loved dearly her husband, her gloriously lovely daughter, Grace, and, of course, her new arrival, Georgie. However, her life seemed to have taken a very marked turn around with the birth of her new son and the death of his twin.

His needs seemed to have become endless, sleeping very fitfully throughout the day *and* night, along with fussiness over his meals, his clothing, and the people around him. It seemed that there was something missing in his life, which tied in closely with his mother's almost depressed feelings. Little James' absence filled their life like no other.

The whole family, Grace included, was bereft of his presence, and nobody felt it more than Georgie although he was unable to express his feelings linguistically. They all considered that that, however, wouldn't always be the case, as he seemed to make the right noises … endlessly. Gurgles, raspberries, screams, physical manifestations related to diet; his repertoire was endlessly varied, leaving everyone grateful for the weekly approach of his first birthday anniversary. Still, that celebration was a little way off yet.

Once Poppy's new book signing had been decided for New York, this McIntyre family would re-emerge in the North Riding ready to make physical preparations, including warning Abigail's parents of their part in looking after Georgie, whom they had not yet seen, for the two weeks Hal, Abigail and Grace would be spending in a significantly foreign land.

They of course were not looking forward to spending time in the cold north of England as they never did where warmth and comfort were concerned. They had been looking forward to visiting Rome, but local issues precluded that stay. One day perhaps…

"It struck me forcibly last evening when we had seen that young man Toby who was introduced to the Booths the other day," Hal said as he dropped the local newspaper next to his chair on the veranda. "Stepson of Jonas Jamieson?"

"Jonas—?" Abigail asked, not sure who he was talking about.

"The chap that was Poppy's acquaintance and relation as a child," Hal explained. "You know, the one with whom George had had a few run-ins. He's dead now."

"Got it!" Abigail responded. "A bad package, so I'm given to understand."

"Should we warn the girls about him?" Hal suggested, feeling it might be his duty at least to give them the heads up. "It could be—"

"None of our business my dear," Abigail reacted without hesitation. "From what you say, at least he wasn't his son, and he seemed a pleasant enough chap. Sarah seemed quite taken with him, if I'm not very much mistaken."

"I wouldn't know about such things," Hal's remark resonated with his wife as he rushed out of the room to attend to Georgie's screaming.

CHAPTER 22

It wasn't an easy task to make a profit, however small, from a farm in the North Riding – or anywhere else for that matter. Ross had done as much research as physically possible, hence the reason for the addition of the café overlooking the milking parlour.

The rabbit venture undertaken by Jim Smallshore was proving to be quite lucrative, with little input necessary to achieve reasonable financial returns. Because of the size of his undertaking, profit returns had become quite noticeable of late. Hence, those unplanned and not small outgoings were always covered, and for this Jim knew he would glory in employment for as long as he needed it.

Ross had arranged to meet Jim out by the pillow mounds, but as he turned the corner by the woods, he wasn't expecting to see the figure sitting on a tree trunk that had been felled by a recent storm.

"George?" he ventured carefully, not really sure that the heavily wrapped figure was in fact his friend and neighbour.

The figure stood up slowly and turned to face Ross. "Recuperating, I assume, in line with doctor's orders?" he quizzed carefully.

"Something like that, old friend," George responded with a wan smile. "Felt like I needed to be out where I belong. Clever idea to breed rabbits. Jim's idea?"

"Aye, it is that," Ross replied. "It's good to si thi. Getting better?"

"Not too bad tha noz," George continued the pleasantries. "Summat I've come to feel, Ross. I know now I've made a significant number of mistakes in my private and professional life, but the latest events have brought me back to reality. One or two things I need to attend to, not the least of which are sorting out mi life and … talking to you and Joseph about mi farm and where it - we – need to be going."

"Do you want to come round for tea early evening, and we'll have a look at what you have to say?" Ross agreed. "Good to see you about, but maybe some more important stuff needs to be discussed to our mutual benefit?"

George agreed and turned to leave as he said in parting, "I hope Poppy's well and enjoying her writing. Please give her my regards when you see her next?"

With that, he was gone.

"George Garside?" Jim Smallshore asked as he approached his rabbit warrens. "Was that really 'im?"

"He looks as if he's bin through t'mill, but it was definitely 'im," Ross replied with a sage nod.

"His farm looks a bit lost since his illness," Jim noticed. "Could do wi' a bit of an upheaval, I think. If he needs a bit on a help, just gi' me a nod. I tell thee summat – I know a few folks as 'ave farms of all shapes and sizes, including hill farms that are on pasture that don't lend themselves to much improvement. I know George has a flock of Herdwicks, but he could perhaps benefit from Blackface or even Cheviots."

"When I see him about more often, I'll have words with

him about not only that, but on suggesting we go back to merging our two places," Ross confided. "Don't say owt to anybody else until I let you know otherwise?"

"Mum's t'word," Jim promised. "There are one or two things you ought to know about mixed farming as well."

"Mixed farming?" Ross queried. "Well, we do sheep and cows."

"Not what mixed farming means, I'm afraid," Jim explained. "It means it's a mixture of crops and pasture livestock. We cover the latter, but not the crop growing. Apparently, specialist farms like cattle and sheep and cash crops as individuals are quite rare. In t'mid 1800s mainly pastoral and livestock keeping were largely current in the North-West, whereas arable and corn growing were largely carried out in the South and East."

"It's good to know, Jim," Ross reacted eagerly. "We have spare land in the valley which I would think might be open to crop growing, whereas the slopes up yonder past the lake and yon forest would remain good for sheep. I need to talk to George and, of course, to our Joseph. I'm sure he will have some qualms about all of this."

***

"We've been thinking largely about our joint future, George," Ross acknowledged as main course dinner plates were cleared away from Boulders Wood's front room dining table.

"One of my main reasons for being here, really, Ross," George joined in to the surprise of his hosts, who cast surprised and concerned glances at each other, "is—"

"Positive reasons, I hope," Joseph reacted, a look of caution etching his features.

"To rewind the last year or two," George went on, ignoring

Joseph's questionable comment.

"If that's what I think it means, it can't come soon enough," Ross reacted, quite excited for him. "Anything to do with a change in your farming … ideas, George?"

This comment seemed to sting his brother into a reaction Joseph didn't seem happy with. "If that means—!" he interrupted sharply, to be stunned into silence by George's startling response.

"I propose we lock together our two farms as we had it before," George's pronouncement caught his host unawares but made Ross smile and relax into his chair. "Also, I will be dividing Garside Farm into two parts: the hill fields will be devoted to sheep, with my Herdwicks joined by Blackface and Cheviot flocks. The lower areas will cultivate arable crops, some of which will be for sale and some to feed *our* animals – both sheep and cattle."

The room fell profoundly silent, with Joseph not expecting what he was hearing, a shocked look heralding his lack of agreement. Ross on the other hand applauded George's unexpected vision, as could be seen by his facial reaction.

"Not sure about that!" Joseph growled.

"Wonderful idea, George!" Ross gushed at the same time. "Although now is not the time to discuss, but I can assure you that it will be shortly."

<hr>

"And if I don't agree with your questionable ideas that George Garside has shared?" Joseph challenged his brother after George had departed.

"Then you are more of a fool than I had thought," Ross returned, a serious look of anger growing in his face. "If you hadn't noticed, farming is going through a serious period of stagnation. My family could tell you that, if only through the amount of time I don't spend with them."

A deeply antagonistic silence descended, leaving Ross aggravated and frustrated in the extreme. They had had their arguments before about modernisation and developments simply because Joseph was comfortable with the present. He didn't ever think about a future that would involve their children. In the present situation their inbred reaction to change in the future would perhaps be selling up and moving to an easier life.

"Here's the thing," Ross began again, his anger now under control. "If you refuse to listen to pragmatic farming sense, we will be moving out – and maybe even taking up partnership with George at Garside farm."

"Now just a minute!" Joseph protested, seeing how serious his brother had become. "We've had disagreements about progress before and have never—"

"Gone that far?" Ross interrupted. "You have never been that intransigent before. When you have arrived at a significantly sensible decision, please let me know."

Turning away and leaving his brother speechless, Ross marched off purposefully to join his wife, Martha, in their quarters in the main building.

～

The front door of Garside Farm's main house rattled loudly as if shaken by a large silverback.

"Hang on a bit!" George shouted as he walked carefully but purposefully slowly because of his physical condition. "Be there in a minute!"

Opening the door carefully, he was surprised to encounter his neighbour, Ross Booth.

"Well now, this is a surprise," George said, a smile dithering around his face. "Please come in, Ross. Mug of tea and a piece of Victoria Sponge?"

"Tea, certainly. Thank you very much," Ross responded with a chortle. "Cake? It all depends on who's baked it."

"I'll have you know that I am a wonderful baker, Ross Booth," George added, a mock hurt look in his face. "But … sister Charity made it."

They both chuckled loudly and headed for the kitchen. Once the tea had mashed and a fist-sized lump of cake appeared on each of two plates, they settled at the bare wooden table under the window looking onto the fields beyond.

"A couple of things really," Ross mumbled through the delicious cake. "I really like your ideas on joining forces again, and … I think your ideas on cropping some of our lower fields have an excellent ring to them."

"And your brother?" George asked warily, not expecting a positive response about *his* views.

"The usual old-fashioned stick in the mud attitude that will have our farms closing down without a future plan," Ross returned, pulling no punches. "I have warned him about my response should he not change his outdated attitude."

"Which would be?" George commented, not expecting what Ross was about to say.

"I threatened I would leave and buy into Garside Farm to work with you on bringing the business up to scratch," Ross explained bluntly. "If he doesn't agree with us, be prepared for my offer to you."

CHAPTER 23

Toby Bott thought he loved what short time he had spent in this lush luxuriant place that he didn't know existed until five days before. His hotel was wonderfully comfortable where he had no need to learn how to do housework or to cook – things his mother had done very well when they lived in Yorkshire's Richmond. The apartment he had been invited to visit by Poppy Spence was in a league of its own.

He had never experienced a façade like these apartments thrust into the outside world. The ones he had seen when he delivered his taxi clients to their front door bore no resemblance. He had never seen let alone travelled in an Otis elevator, nor had he imagined he would ever be living within spitting distance of such a wonderfully warm and invitingly calm sea.

Not knowing whether he was now living in a real world, all he could do was stare at such attention-grabbing features before he was able to tear himself away.

"Hello Toby," Poppy greeted him as she opened her grandpa's door upon hearing its bell. "Please come in."

Bemused by the beauty of this young lady before him and the room into which she had ushered him, all he could do was gaze at these new surroundings in awe.

143

Even though introductions were quick and easy, Toby still felt a little overcome by the company because they were all part of the same family, and he was … an outsider. The only member of this family he felt at ease with was … Poppy, the one he had met before anyone else. Consequently, he gravitated towards her more than any of the others.

"Don't I know you?" Hal challenged the newcomer as he and his family settled to the gathering.

"I don't … think so," Toby Bott responded, a slightly puzzled look crossing his brow.

"I've a feeling that we might be related in some way," Hal persisted despite the warning looks from his wife. "I am Poppy's cousin once removed, on the male side, and as far as I am aware, you, my friend, are a product of the McIntyre family from__"

A loud screech from Hal and Abigail's new son silenced the room, causing Abigail to gather him quickly to her bosom.

"Hal!" she beckoned her husband, a seriously warning look inhabiting her face. "It's getting late, so I think we ought to retire and put our children to bed."

With that the McIntyre family bade their farewell and left.

"Well done, Hal!" Abigail chastised him as they entered their own abode only moments later. "The relationship between Toby and the McIntyres needs to be kept … away from the company."

"Why, might I ask?" he responded, not understanding the subterfuge that had just raised its head. "Is it—?"

"Contentious to say the least," she urged. "Because of his seriously 'close' relation to the family through their male side, it would be a good idea to leave well alone."

"You mean … Joss?" Hal went on quietly as he snecked the apartment door from the inside.

"Enough!" she countered sharply. "To take it further could cause serious problems."

⌒

"A part of me, then, thinks your brother may well take exception to our suggestions," George responded to Ross's comments about their two farms. "I would very much look forward to working with you again though, Ross."

"Mixed farming makes absolute sense in the present volatile environment," Ross added. "It would give us greater control of our markets. We could—"

A hefty banging at the front door silenced the two men, causing them to cast puzzled glances at each other. Imagine their surprise when Joseph McIntyre strolled into the room, a slight smile curling his mouth corners, and a very sharp breeze snapping at his heals.

"Before you both say anything, you need to hear me out," he urged before they even had chance to sit down.

"Good afternoon to you too," Ross uttered his slightly sarcastic greeting.

"I've given a lot of thought to what Ross has said about our way forward with both farms," Joseph started, his flat hand facing his audience as a sign not to interrupt. "I have to say that I don't possess the same breadth of perception as you two because to me a farm's role has always been a way of producing high quality meat for our customers."

"And that has always been the case," Ross agreed.

"Times have changed though, as they do according to need and desire," George added quickly.

"So, I have to agree with you both," Joseph reacted slowly. "We seem to have a lot of flat land that produces a hell of a lot of … grass, and nowt else. Perhaps…"

"We might be able to change that to cultivating arable crops…" George suggested.

"Some of which could be used to feed our livestock…" Ross jumped in.

"And some for the open market?" Joseph finished as he sat back on the settee with a huge sigh.

"We have a deal!" Ross and George added in chorus as they, too, sat back in their chairs, a huge grin on their face.

"Next steps?" Joseph asked.

"An assessment of how much spare land we have, and research into what we need to grow according to market demand," Ross answered without hesitation.

"And what we might need for our own use with our livestock," George acknowledged. "Both sheep and cows, bearing in mind meat and milk production."

"We also need to decide if we will have enough staff to manage all we need to do," Ross suggested sagely. "We have enough … for now, but when we increase our production, what then?"

"Do we need to make the joining of Garside Farm and Boulders Wood official, with legal agreements?" George wondered, not too sure what he felt.

"I would have preferred a return to our agreement in place before the split," Joseph suggested. "If we need to rationalise it, we can discuss matters later. We ought to discuss matters any time soon. Agreed?"

"Good decision, Brother," Ross congratulated Joseph as they reached Boulders Wood's noisy driveway. "The only sensible thing to do. This will make us the largest farm in the North Riding."

"And will stabilise supplies and costs for some time," Joseph agreed.

The living room at Boulders Wood was unusually quiet and empty which Ross noticed immediately.

"Quiet in here today?" he noted, looking around their enormous front room for their youngsters to leap out at them playing hide and seek.

"They're probably at our cottage having some tea and cake," Joseph countered. "They always play games."

"That's just made me realise that we have some sponge cake in the kitchen's pantry," Ross added gleefully. "I could murder a mug of tea and…"

"Stay where you are don't come any nearer!" a threatening voice rang out as they stepped into the kitchen.

Lilly Victoria and Martha were gagged and roped to two chairs, with the children herded into the corner by the back door. Two hooded men bearing pistols confronted the brothers from behind the chairs, knowing what Ross was capable of.

"Take one step forward and I shoot one of your women," one of the men uttered menacingly. "Take two steps and one of your kids gets it as well. These guns *are* loaded."

"What do you want, scumbag?" Ross uttered menacingly.

"Your money or your – their – life!" the same thug replied with a sneer.

CHAPTER 24

Enjoyable though it was, the time spent with Poppy and her family left Toby with a few qualms and feelings of uncertainty.

He knew his *supposed* heritage but why would that supposition be of any interest to the likes of Hal McIntyre? Toby knew any link with Joss McIntyre was a distant possibility only, as he was aware of his mother's life before he had been born; a lifestyle that few would have welcomed into their history.

Abigail McIntyre's reaction to her husband's near aggression on his attempted revelations also seemed to be an over-reaction of something that was valueless to him. More important would be his relationship with Jonas Jamieson that could have been easily misinterpreted.

If people wished to lay links on his shoulders that were unproductive and unprovable then so be it. He intended to live his own life no matter what they thought. At last, he had discovered where he wanted to live, and Jonas had left him the wherewithal to at least partially find it. He had no intention of researching how Jonas had come by those finances, but he would enjoy what they could do to support, at least in part, the rest of his life. He was sad and disappointed that his mother had been prevented from sharing it with him.

An urgent rattling of his hotel bedroom door drew him from these deep thoughts.

Opening the door very carefully – a caution he had learned in his previous life – he was greeted by the beautiful form of a young lady.

"Good morning; Sarah isn't it?" he reacted with joy. "Instead of entering the male boudoir of a swish holiday hotel, would you join me for a spot of lunch in the dining room downstairs?"

"I should be delighted," she reacted with a giggle at the comment. They made for the stairs as his room was on a reasonable floor, ready to grace a busy restaurant with their presence.

Once they had ordered they started to engage in pleasant fripperies that he had never indulged in with a young and beautiful woman before.

"I hope you weren't offended by Hal's comments last evening," she commented gently, her rich Antipodean accent engaging his attention completely.

"Not at all," he replied with a dismissive wave of his hand and an engaging smile. "Unfortunately, I had no control over the manner of my conception nor my ancestry. Any comments or concerns from anybody would cause me no harm at all. I was very glad to have been introduced to such wonderful people – you and your sister above all."

"We – you and I – share the same feelings," Sarah added, warming to her companion. "We can't be held responsible for our entry to this world. We can only enhance our place in it."

"We certainly share the same views on that one," Toby agreed eagerly. "What are you going to do now you're here? Stay with your sister? Buy a place of your own?"

"I'm staying with my father, Ross, for now because I haven't found anything I would be happy to call my own," Sarah reacted unsure of what was to come next for her. "I've already travelled the world to find him, and I find it difficult to say I don't want to live with or close to him anymore. My real mother died a while ago, and I should like to say the same about my real dad when his time arrives."

"My real mother died in dodgy circumstances a short while ago, and I have only a disjointed view on who my real father was," he responded. "Consequently, I have neither current family nor ancestors I could count, which has always been the case."

He continued to explain the circumstances surrounding his mother's end which she listened to in silence, an obvious sense of disquiet surrounding his explanation.

"I am so sorry," she said quietly, reaching out to hold his hand in comfort, which he accepted with gratitude. Although he didn't express such feelings to her, he felt drawn to her as a person as she bore similar sentiments to his. She was the sort of woman he felt he could spend a lot of time with.

***

"Money or my life, eh?" Ross responded with a sardonic smile. "What's keeping you? Time to make a choice?"

A significant show of growing disquiet began to move slowly across the thug's face, not believing what he was hearing. Cocking his pistol, he raised it slowly at his adversary's chest, trying to persuade him that he meant what he was saying.

"If I were you, mate, I would put down the gun and give up as there is a twelve-gauge shotgun pointing at your back, and—" Ross warned the miscreant.

"And you think you can bluff me with your stupid words?"

the masked man cajoled with a derisory snigger. Taking aim directly at Ross, he paused, about to pull the trigger when he heard the ominous click of a locking gun barrel behind him.

He swung around, head and pistol poised, cocked hammer ready to fire to be met by a blast that hit him in the chest, knocking his now dead and limp body to Ross's feet. The second thug swung round with his gun primed.

"Feeling lucky, Stupid?" came the response from the newcomer.

It was George, a twelve-gauge shotgun, stock against his shoulder, the barrel pointing at the thug, level with his own keen eye.

"I have a second loaded barrel that will wipe you from the face of this earth if you don't drop your pistol," he went on.

Once untied, Lilly Victoria and Martha comforted their children as Ross secured the criminal.

"George! How on earth did you know?" Joseph gasped, wringing his hand in gratitude.

"I noticed as I passed the back door on my way to let you know about something I had forgotten, through the hazy glass panel, two large shadowy figures that weren't you," he explained. "Realising they shouldn't be there, I nipped back to the farm for my twelve gauge, squeezed silently through the door into the scullery – and the rest is history."

"I've telephoned the police, and they'll be here about … now," Martha acknowledged, a tremor in her voice, as she heard the police vehicle rushing towards the front door.

"Not that keen on miscreants, eh, Mr Garside?" the police inspector noted with a shake of his head. "Can I ask you to hand me the gun? I'll need to take this as evidence, but I'm sure Mr McIntyre and Mr Booth will be prepared to provide corroborating evidence as to why it was necessary to dispatch one of these miscreants.”

“Self-defence, Inspector,” George offered. “He was about to shoot *me*. Been poorly enough recently without having to manage with a bullet in mi body!”

“Any idea why they were here?” the inspector asked. “Apart from the obvious?”

“The obvious, I should think,” Joseph responded with a non-committal shrug. “As they threatened violence if we didn’t give them money, I would imagine that that was the prime reason.”

“I don’t know yet, but I believe there must have been some other reason,” Ross countered. “*That* one seems to be a bit too obvious to me.”

CHAPTER 25

Although the French Riviera maintained its undimin-
ished appeal for all those who had been visitors since
its early foundation, there were those that didn't stay, for
whatever reason. Once Edward, Prince of Wales, had risen to
the throne upon his mamma's death, he almost immediately
took up a summer residence at the opposite side of the country in Biarritz. No reason, no concern other than his choice.
His Mamma, until her death, spent significant amounts of
summertime in Cimiez, a part of Nice graced by Ross Senior
and *his* offspring.

Poppy, of course, had had her friend and agent as her
teacher for much of her time in his and Abigail's company
dealing with the presentation of her wonderfully whimsical
novel *Faithfully Yours* to the world. This had become a way of
life for them all, including Hal and Abigail's young daughter,
Grace, for whom trips to France, New York and many places
in Britain had become an adventure within which no-one else
of her age had been indulged.

Although they might be deciding upon the next country
within which to launch Poppy's next venture into the printed
word, they would have to be careful where that might take them.

During Edward's reign in the very early part of the twentieth century, there had developed a few political rumblings concerning problems between certain nations. However, these hadn't cast worries in the direction of most ordinary citizens who lived *their* lives according to *their* wishes.

Ross Senior and his twin daughters were such people, with Ross undoubtedly deciding to finish his worthy life where he had settled. Not too sure about Rosie and Sarah though. They had planned to settle where he was … for the time being.

There had been a second Boer War in South Africa involving the British Empire which lasted three years or so, but nothing to involve or worry folks on the French Riviera. Hal, of course, had charted all of such activities involving his countryfolk.

"We have to be extremely careful where we go because of the possible flare-ups that might occur through historical bases," Hal would warn, knowing where that might happen in certain places. "So, Paris I would think not. New York, perhaps. The two places most likely to be successful might be London, one of the North of England's major cities, or even here on the French Riviera."

"How about here first," Abigail suggested. "It would give me and Georgie time to recuperate, followed by our return to England? Poppy?"

Poppy was quiet for a few minutes, seeming to give the question a good deal of careful thought.

"Poppy?" Abigail asked quietly, wondering what was going through her head.

"I hope this doesn't sound ungrateful," Poppy reacted cautiously. "But I don't think I want to launch either in America or … here. I think I'd just like us to wander back to England and … home. Don't get me wrong! I love it here and it has been a fabulous adventure, but I'm strangely missing the old country."

"So, a bit longer here and then off to Richmond in the North Riding?" Hal responded. "I've a feeling my wife and the nippers would like the same too. Abigail? Gracie?"

That was met with sagely nodding heads and Grace's arms wrapped around her father's neck in obvious agreement.

"I feel like I'm missing the English cool at this time of year," Grace stated wisely. "It would be exciting to go back home to go to school and to make a few friends, perhaps."

Trust Grace to have thought it all through maturely!

"We are in your hands, then, my lovely," Hal said with a smile to his wife, wrapping his arms around her unprotesting body.

Toby had no such qualms concerning his short time on the French Riviera. He loved the area; he adored living on the Mediterranean front; his favourite part was … the very warm climate – even in the winter. His mother, Jenny Bott, would have loved it. If they had left when he wanted, she would still have been here, enjoying life with him.

Unfortunately, he would have to spend his time on his own doing things he loved to do. Or would he? He loved the company of Poppy, though, the beautiful young lady from Richmond. Would she, however, reciprocate his developing feelings for her, and would he feel confident enough to share how he felt?

A sharp knocking at his bedroom door drew his attention from his deep thoughts. It was the young man from Reception at the front of the hotel.

"Sorry to disturb you, monsieur, but there is a young lady

asking to see you," the young man explained. "Her name is Mademoiselle Booth."

Toby was surprised, puzzled and pleased that she had called to see him. Whatever she wanted was irrelevant because her company was all he wanted. To share, perhaps, part of a day with her without having to have a taxi driver's conversation with her.

Putting on a decent jacket to show that he did have a modicum of style, he locked the door behind him and headed for the flight of ornate, partially carpeted stairs to the foyer, excitement growing with each mahogany step trodden.

"Miss Booth?" he questioned the young lady whose back was towards him, as he approached the softly furnished easy chairs in the foyer. As she turned around on his greeting, he realised the mistake he had made immediately. "Miss *Sarah* Booth?"

"Hello Mr *Toby* Bott," she responded with a smile. "Just Sarah will do, if that's all right with you."

"Sarah," he replied, "A beautifully warm and sunny day. Would you like to go for a stroll along the front?"

"The front of what?" she returned, something of a puzzled look inhabiting her beautiful Australian face.

"The Yorkshire word for the walk along by the sea," he explained. "To be followed by dinner? Again, another Yorkshire word for 'lunch'."

"A strange language you Yorkshire folk speak!" Sarah answered. "I should be delighted to work up an appetite for 'dinner'."

They both burst into gentle peals of laughter as they made for the hotel's front door on their way to the Mediterranean's 'front', hopefully to enjoy each other's company on a very warm and sunny morning stroll.

Chapter 26

"It was entirely self-defence, Inspector Shaw," George explained in the police station.

"Please tell me again why you were carrying a twelve-gauge double-barrelled shot gun," the inspector asked. "Do you usually carry one of those – lethal – weapons around with you? Something I am sure ordinary, normal citizens don't do."

"Joseph McIntyre and his brother, Ross Booth, had been to see me at my farm to discuss ways of improving our joint productivity following months of quietness," George began his explanation clearly. "We had arrived at an agreement on several suggestions, after which they left. It occurred to me that we hadn't discussed a time scale, so I set off – a matter of minutes away – to Boulders Wood to ascertain their important thoughts. Passing their kitchen's glass door, I saw two shadowy figures the other side of the frosted glass of the door that weren't Joseph and Ross, waving about what looked like pistols.

"I hurried back to my farm to collect my shotgun to bear as a warning on my return," George went on. "Sneaking in through the kitchen door, I could see that one of them was about to shoot Ross. I intervened, warning him that he should drop his pistol. He turned to me and was about to shoot …

and the rest is history. As I said before … self-defence.”

“That corroborates what Mr McIntyre and Mr Booth have said separately,” the policeman agreed. “The two blackguards, one of whom is now no longer alive, have been known to us for some time, being part of a violent, robbing gang we have been chasing for a while. I am quite convinced that had you not dropped him, you wouldn’t be sitting here talking to me now.”

“The other one, Inspector Shaw?” George added quietly.

“Behind bars where he will stay for a very long time,” the inspector added, closing the file in front of him on his desk. “Thank you for your time, Mr Garside. If we need anything else from you, we’ll be in touch.”

George sighed deeply as he made his way out of the police station, to be met by Ross at the pavement’s side.

“Everything all right, Old Chap?” Ross asked quietly.

“Couldn’t be better,” George responded. “Except that I’m thirsty and starving.”

“Mary’s Pantry is just down the road,” Ross suggested. “Feel like a mug of tea and summat to eat? My treat as you’re the reason I am still here talking to you.”

“Hello Ross and George,” Mary greeted the two as they sat at a table in the window. “What can I get you? Your usual?”

“I’m afraid it’s several months since we had our ‘usual’ here with you, Mary,” Ross replied. “How—?”

“Beef sandwich, large piece of Victoria Sponge and mug of tea,” she responded accurately without pause, but with a self-satisfied smile creeping across her face.

“I am astounded!” George gasped in amazed wonder. “I could just—”

He was interrupted by Mary-Jane carrying a tray of food and drink out to their table, forcing the two men to gasp in joy that their deep hunger was about to be assuaged. Their table had been covered with plates filled with food they had been offered verbally by Mary; food that made their mouth water and dribble mentally and physically.

"You always tickle my memory with stuff I had forgotten some time before, Ross," George offered as he tucked in to this gorgeously delicious food. "It reminds me that I need to get out more and not spend all the time I am awake working."

"You need not only to get out, my friend," Ross agreed. "What you have to remember is that you have a nipper the same as I do, and they are the best catalyst for enjoying what you have."

"*You* also have my sister to keep you on the straight and narrow, don't forget," George retorted.

"How could I?" his friend returned with a guffaw. "Martha is very good at doing just that, as is your boss sister, Lilly Victoria."

George burst into hearty laughter, no doubt remembering the control he was under with four older sisters watching over and looking after him. The youngest two were still his guardians to this day, bearing in mind what he had been through over the last few years. What other man could have coped with the loss of two wives, one prospective wife, one four-year-old child plus one other stillborn?

Entering his fourth month living on the French Riviera in a hotel he adored allowed Toby Bott to decide that that was where he would like to live … permanently. He had decided that it may well be time to take up employment because his 'fortune', achieved through the sale of his house in Richmond and the pot of money left by his mother and stepfather, Jonas Jamieson, would not last forever. He still had a sterling amount residing in his bank account, however, but there were several things he wanted to achieve. One of those was remaining close to his lady friend with a view to claiming her for his own in the near future.

Should he ask her for her hand in the hope she might agree to become *his* forever? He had practised asking her, on his own in his hotel room, but reality was unfortunately quite daunting. Would she ever consider a young man of such lowly status – no history, no future as yet, no real standing in their society, and above all, no source of income.

It had taken him a reasonable length of time to arrive at the decision that he wanted to live on the Riviera permanently, and during that time he had observed the function of Taxi firms within that area. He had noticed, too, that they drove on the wrong side of the road, which meant he would have to practise driving before he could set up business as a taxi driver.

The car he needed to choose to be able to achieve his aim reasonably well couldn't be the one donated to him by Jonas because its steering wheel was on the wrong side, and … he had sold it. To achieve his next driving goal, he needed urgently to seek advice. But, from whom? His only choice was to ask Sarah's dad, Ross Booth. As a driver himself, he would know.

"Sarah?" Toby asked his friend at their usual luncheon restaurant. "I need to ask you a question."

"Oh, yes?" she replied eagerly. "Fire away. I'm all ears."

He felt he had to refrain from making the obvious comment to that answer, but said, "Would it be all right to ask your father for advice on a matter close to my heart?"

"I should think so," she responded, an excited smile displaying the dimples in her cheeks and moving closer to him. "What is it you'd like to know?"

"Well, what sort of a car should I buy to start my own taxi business hereabouts?" he added slowly.

"Oh, is that all you need to know?" she returned, her smile disappearing immediately in disappointment.

"Sorry," he muttered, more than a little confused by her answer. "Were you expecting me to ask something else?"

"I don't know really," she answered a little downheartedly with no sign of her delighted expression from earlier.

Perhaps she had something else on her mind that she wanted him to say; something of a more *personal* nature that might involve *her*? His heart began to beat a little quicker, thinking about the question that he might feel happier asking. His mind began to race as he reached across the table to grasp her lovely hand.

"Would you have preferred me to ask him about … us?" he stuttered as his face turned a pale crimson from embarrassment at realising he was being presumptuous. "I'm sorry. I shouldn't have said that. I—"

"That's just what I wanted you to say," she blurted out, grasping his hand eagerly.

"I would love to … marry you, Sarah," he gasped. "But I'm not rich and would have to earn money to live…"

"You may not be, but I am," she encouraged him. "I never knew what love was about, Toby … before I met you, and now I should love nothing more than to—"

"Marry *me*?" he added quickly.

"Are you asking?" she said, a giggle rising in her throat.

"Well, yes, I'm asking," he retorted a little more confidently.

"Then that's two questions you have to put to father," she encouraged, sitting on his lap, much to the surprise of the other folks in the restaurant. "Come on! Why are we waiting?"

CHAPTER 27

"Hello? Poppy? Is that you?" her father, Tommy Spence, shouted on his telephone call to the French Riviera.

"It is, Father, but there is no need to shout," she advised with a giggle. "I'm only a few miles away, and telephone machines are becoming better very quickly. Most countries in the world now have them."

"We've only just got to know that you have a couple of Australian aunts on your Grandpa Ross's side," Tommy queried, calming his voice a little.

"Indeed, yes," Poppy agreed. "Two aunts I didn't know I had. Rosie and Sarah are identical twins who discovered each other only when they arrived in England/the French Riviera separately. Can't tell them apart. They even sound like each other."

"Not seen you for quite a while," he rejoined. "But I'm sure you'll be having a wonderful time launching your books."

"Beginning to miss home, so we won't be here much longer," Poppy said. "We'll be back on the Train Bleu in the very near future, when Abigail is fit to travel."

"Abigail?" he questioned in surprise. "Not unwell, I hope?"

Poppy explained the reasons for their lengthy stay before she took her leave.

"Your dad, stepmother and half siblings all right?" Ross Senior asked, genuinely interested in their well-being. "Two siblings now?"

"That's the news," she went on causing him to gasp in surprise. "They have another one on the way."

"Might you be interested in producing at some time?" Rosie asked.

"Not really," Poppy responded. "My only productions, I feel, will be my stories. Besides, I have no-one to engineer children with."

Said with a slight quiver in her voice that obviously those that knew her recognised, she felt her family-producing days were drawing to a close. She would have been delighted, however, to have had a lovely man with whom to share her exciting life.

At one time, George would have been the ideal choice, but he wanted that sort of relationship long before Poppy did. Unable to wait for the appropriate time, he rushed into two marriages and one almost-marriage stupidly. Was George just now a memory, or was there still a chance they might achieve what George felt they were meant to do? She thought not.

She was still young, with plenty of time to find the right partner...

***

"I know nothing about buying motor cars in this country," Toby uttered, feeling more than a little out of his depth. "I had the Landaulette bought for me in England by my mother's partner, and that was very popular with customers. And, of course, here they all have steering wheels on the left!"

"This week I'll speak to some of my closest contacts who know about these things," Ross Senior offered freely. "Let's see – it's Sunday today, so you should have your answer by the end of the week. To your second question, my answer is unequivocally 'Yes'."

A look of confusion began to settle in his eyes at this strange and unexpected response from Grandpa Ross.

"Your second question concerned your future hoped for relationship with my daughter, Sarah," Ross went on. "That is obvious. I know she would be more than happy to have you for her husband … and I would be delighted for you to become my son-in-law."

"You won't believe how happy that makes me feel," Toby said quietly, a look of ecstasy in his face.

"Oh yes I will!" Ross replied fervently. "I was unable to have my one true love – Poppy's mother, Annie. It's *that* that persuaded me to emigrate to the Antipodes. I wasn't able to cement a lasting relationship because of what I had lost and left."

"Must have been devastating," Toby reacted, a sad look decorating his face. "I've lost people I loved, but never anything like that."

"Sarah will be here in a short while," Ross rejoined. "You can ask her what she thinks then. Either in private or openly."

"I would love family to be around because the only family I've ever had was my mother," Toby rejoined. "She's now no longer with us, and so I would love to have your family as mine."

"Wonderful," Ross acknowledged with a grin and a hand-shake. "It's all up to you two. Whatever she says goes. Sounds like a click of the door now. Perhaps that's … Sarah!" he greeted his daughter with a shout and a hug as she entered the living room.

"Rosie!" he added after a moment's pause, noticing her

entry to the room a short while after her sister.

"Poppy!" he went on again, not having expected there to be almost a full house as she joined the throng.

When they had greeted their father/grandfather appropriately, they all sat down talking about where they had been and what they had been doing for the morning. When quiet stole into the room, before the girls slid off to make coffee and tea, Ross drew their attention.

"We have something very exciting and lovely to announce," he started slowly. "Toby?"

Turning a very slightly embarrasses pink, he stood up slowly as all surprised faces turned towards him.

Giving a slightly nervous cough to clear the throat of an invisible and imagined blockage, his eyes fixed on the woman of his dreams.

"Ross and I have had a lengthy discussion about something close to my heart," he started. "The upshot is that he has given his whole-hearted approval for me to ask … Sarah," he turned towards Ross's daughter and said, "will you do me the honour of becoming my bride?"

He dropped slowly to one knee and drew out of his pocket an ornate violet box that he opened to reveal a gold ring with a huge solitaire diamond at its centre of around five carats weight. Flashing luxuriously as the light caught its exquisite cut, Toby drew it out of the box and offered it to the woman of his choice.

The look of surprised joy on her face betrayed the happiness she felt as she rushed from the settee to fling her arms about his neck, ending up in a pile on the floor together, surrounded by the mirth and joy of all there.

"Of course I'll marry you!" she urged, picking herself up from the floor, the ring settling nicely on her marriage finger.

The young man stood up next to her, whereupon she threw herself upon him again, tears streaming down her face in utter joy.

"He does have my permission to sweep you off your feet, Sweet Sarah," Ross butted in, to the laughter of all in the room.

<hr>

"Well, that's a turn up!" Hal blustered when he learned about what had happened. "Very nice for him and for her, but if he wanted to earn a proper wage as a taxi man, he would take himself off to Paris where there are thousands on the roads."

"Then it's a good job he's here," Abigail responded firmly. "Not as much competition here as there. So, surely, they'll be better off in the long run?"

Hal was a clever manufacturer and manager of facts and figures, and the history of everything that belonged to or had grown within the world they inhabited. However, he found reality a little challenging to say the least and would have been better sticking to what he felt most comfortable with.

"Will we be going home soon, Daddy?" Grace asked. "Only, the one or two friends I had when we lived in Yorkshire have moved on to secondary school, and now I have none."

"Hal?" Abigail asked.

"I have booked carriages on the Train Bleu for the day after tomorrow ... tentatively," Hall explained. "If you are well enough to travel, Abigail?"

"Have you booked for Poppy, too?" Grace asked again. "I think she ought to accompany us on our lengthy journey."

"Indeed," Hal responded with a broad smile. "Although *we* need to return to our home in the North Riding, Poppy was the main instigator of our journey."

"And we need to get back with your new little brother,"

Abigail added. "Don't you think, Grace?"

"I do," Grace reacted. "There are all sorts of English things I have to show him before he can understand the difference between us and the others who live in … Europe. I also need to get back to spending proper money – pounds and pence and florins and crowns, oh and half crowns. What is half a crown, Daddy?"

"It's two shillings and sixpence, my little one," Hal shot back at her immediately.

C H A P T E R   2 8

"We can always publicise your new book, so it is available for purchase in New York and Paris," Hal stated categorically as the train clickety-clacked its way from London northwards.

"We ought to speak to Jenny Wilton, our publisher, about our next steps," Abigail replied, nursing her son, Georgie, and trying to persuade him to take his milk from her breast.

"Not having a lot of success there," Hal butted in. "Solid food soon?"

"Have a look in my bag next to where Grace is sitting," Abigail suggested. "The one with the blue handles."

"Will we be home soon, Daddy?" Grace joined in the conversation, not taking her eyes from the countryside flashing by. "I've seen all this ... countryside before, and I'm getting a bit—"

"Bored by it all?" Poppy interjected, knowing how she felt. Been there! Done that! want a change! Thank you very much! "Can I help you in any way?"

"Poppy?" Grace asked a short while later. "I think I'd like to learn how to write a story about my life. Would it be possible for you to help me?"

"Of course it would, Grace," Poppy responded happily, a knowing smile growing. "I have some paper and an ink quill or two. If we sit in yonder corner, we could make a few notes and begin."

They shuffled about, moving non-useful articles out of the way so they could sit together side-by-side next to the window table. Once everything had been sorted, a profound silence cascaded over them, interrupted only by the occasional clack of metal wheel over metal rail point. Hal closed his eyes, along with his son, Georgie, on his lap.

Abigail breathed a huge sigh of relief to be able to sit in peace and quiet on her own with her thoughts. Part of her 'self' time she spent in reminiscence over the last ten years or so, as a person that forgot little of what had happened during this time. Hal McIntyre had changed her life totally for the better, allowing her to usher her life before him and her little darling Grace to the depths of her subconscious. She loved her present time helping her close friend, Poppy, to achieve her desires as an excellent writer of popular fiction. Abigail valued her as close to family as she could have wished.

There had been times in her past life upon which she had no desire to dwell, that she hadn't been pleased to have experienced. Should she take herself back to when she had wanted to become a writer herself? That held no desires for her now. Whatever had occurred in her early life needed to stay there … forever.

"Mammy! Mammy!" Grace warned as the train slowed. "York is about to thrust itself back into our lives."

"Back into our *life*, Grace dear," Hal corrected her popular grammatical mistake. "We only have one life each that we all share as a family."

My word! How that soon-to-be nine-year-old had grown!

Nine going on nineteen! Her life alone had been an exciting adventure that the whole family had shared. How she had matured beyond her years even in the six months they had been resident on the French Riviera! Now learning from the best how to write stories that anyone would want to read.

Their train from York to Richmond took an age, chugging along more slowly than anything they had experienced on the route to and from the Mediterranean.

"Who are all these people?" Poppy gasped as they passed cars, carriages and walkers along the driveway to the house at Boulders Wood. "Are we at the right place? There was never a child's playground here before we left for France. Swings, roundabouts and a large … slide? What's going on?"

Having paid the taxi driver and wandered into the living room of the cottage Poppy used to inhabit to drop off their luggage, she was amazed to see how more spick and clean and warm it felt than when she had left it a long time before.

"I think we need to call in at the house to—" she began to say, to be cut short by an unexpected intruder.

"George?" she went on, stricken by the figure coming out of the kitchen.

Straight, clean-shaven, well dressed and good-lookingly healthy, she was shocked by the vision that confronted her.

"George … how—?" she stammered, unable to take in what she was seeing.

"Poppy," he said, marching across purposefully to embrace her. "More beautiful than ever. Hal. Abigail. And this lovely young lady must be … Grace."

"Daddy!" a young girl's voice rang out as a child followed him out of the kitchen. It was his daughter, Maisie, who seemed to have shot up since the last time Poppy had seen her.

Poppy was astounded to hear how different George sounded from the last time they had spoken. He was more … relaxed … forthright … normal. And his appearance…

"Like a fairground out there, eh?" George ventured. "And very different from the last time you were here. Ross and Joseph decided they needed to do something … add something … to the old farm to attract customers to visit. Hence, they have had installed a … café where people can visit for an afternoon's break. High class drinks and snacks. Where else can you get such … delicacies, not far from here?"

"Mary's Pantry by any chance?" Poppy ventured.

"Shall we go across and have a look?" George offered. "You'll be shocked … in a good way."

"Mary!" Poppy exclaimed joyfully as they entered the café, rushing to embrace the friend she had known since birth. "I knew it!

"And Mary-Jane?" Poppy reacted on seeing her coming from the kitchen with a tray laden with goodies, China crockery and … a steaming silver teapot.

"Where did you get such a wonderful idea?" Abigail asked in awe. "Cafés are becoming commonplace wherever we have travelled. But an activity park for young children – very clever. Our Grace can't stay off the swings and slide. Very safe but exciting at the same time."

"Idea for a café came from Ross with a significant amount of help from Mary," Lilly Victoria replied. "But the idea for a little activity park was entirely Mary's idea."

"Has it made any difference though?" Poppy asked pointedly.

"In what respect do you mean?" George asked quietly.

"Has it brough in any more revenue, for example?" she explained. "Or was it just a … trial … something different?"

"We have almost recouped the original outlay," Ross rejoined as he re-entered the living room from the front door. "Once we have a full first year's trade, we should about break even on staff and materials, according to Mary. After that, the sky's the limit."

"Feel like a walk to the playground?" George asked Poppy as he made for the door.

Standing up to follow him, she made it to the door just after George.

Although quite bright and sunny, the weather felt nothing like Southern France and must have been several degrees cooler. Fortunately for her, George had warned her about the temperature as the end of this reasonably pleasant day started to close in.

"Have you fully recovered from your illness?" Poppy asked tentatively as they strolled along.

"It was touch and go really for some time," he responded after a few moments of painful silence. "Until I realised it was useless glorifying in my misery. From then it's been slow progress with family help."

"And now?" she ventured not wishing to reemphasise what he had been through.

"Every day is a new experience for me, as long as I have family ready to hand," he acknowledged firmly. "I have no intention of revisiting the depths of despair that enveloped and almost took me during that bleak time.

"Enough of that," he suggested after a few moments of pregnant silence. "How are things with you and your writing? It is good to see you. Will you be staying here for long?"

"For good, I think," Poppy returned quietly. "I will be doing the occasional book signing perhaps but hopefully will be moving back into my cottage certainly for the foreseeable future."

CHAPTER 29

"We have to be very careful about visiting Paris and New York again as I mentioned in Nice the other day," Hal warned as they ate a hearty breakfast in their new home in Richmond.

"Floods and violence and the like?" Abigail observed as she tucked in to her lovely dish of porridge and honey her husband had made. Her thoughts weren't really on what he had to say. Her porridge always took precedence over all unnecessary conversations. She couldn't bear to have it go cold!

Silence fell except for the sound of spoon against porridge dish, and the chomping of crisp fresh fruit.

"Now," she said when breakfast had been consigned to a delighted and delightful memory – until the next time. "Poppy should be the one to be consulted on that one. I believe she wants to stay locally from now on."

"Locally?" he puzzled, a frown almost disfiguring his face. "What does that mean?"

"It means that we will have to do our research on bookshops and book sellers closer to home with, perhaps, the odd foray to London, maybe," she offered thoughtfully, now looking at him eyeball to eyeball. "How difficult would that be?"

"Much easier that we now have a telephone," Hal suggested quickly. "Less expensive, too. No lengthy journeys or hotel stays or … ordering and having books delivered to the next signing!"

"I think our Grace is becoming – what shall we say? – a little less enthusiastic about travelling too," Abigail retorted. "And, of course, we now have our little Georgie. Travelling to somewhere reasonably local would make it much easier for us as well."

"Perhaps we need to contact Poppy to discuss the next one – launch of *And Now?*" Hal urged. "The sooner the better as shops and printers are getting busier and, consequently, more expensive."

"Give her – and us – a few days rest and recuperation and then we'll take on an all-out onslaught," Abigail rejoined. "Has she finished typing the manuscript yet?"

"My manuscript has been finished and ready for some time for Jenny Wilton to cast her discerning eye over," Poppy replied to Abigail's tentative question. "I've also had significant ideas about my next series of books."

"Interesting," Abigail commented, a very significant look gathering in her face. "Cup of tea? Sit down and tell me more."

"*And Now?* will be the last of two," Poppy offered thoughtfully. "I'm thinking of setting the next stories in the early eighteenth to late nineteenth centuries – from George I to early Victorian times; a time which saw this Hanoverian family rule for over a hundred and forty years. I have come to love history, and so the stories will be fiction but accurately historically based."

"Well now!" Abigail gasped in awed wonder. "Times of

Jane Austen, Lord Byron, Percy Bysshe Shelley, John Keats, William Wordsworth, Samuel Taylor Coleridge, Elizabeth Barrett Browning, The Brontë sisters, George Eliot otherwise known as Mary Ann Evans. For you to carry on the literary magic like no-one else has before you, eh?"

"I'm sure there will be more than a bit of influence levied on my historical writing," Poppy gloried, loving her historical forebears like no other.

"When will you be starting that, pray?" Abigail queried.

"Already started," Poppy replied with a pert smile. "I have several pages of notes following on from my research throughout the period."

"Exciting stuff," Hal's gruff voice intervened as he settled with a steaming mug of tea and a sweat meal biscuit. "Do you know that these biscuits I am consuming now were invented by two Scottish doctors as a support for stomachs that were suffering with acid flux, in the 1890s? They were often called 'digestive' biscuits because they aided the digestive system. One of the ingredients was sodium bicarbonate which possessed ant-acid properties. First manufactured by McVitie in 1892."

"You can always trust *my* husband to come up with disparate interesting – but irrelevant – factual matters," Abigail rejoined, to the hearty guffaws of their friend Poppy.

"One of the reasons he is such an interesting man," Poppy went on, wiping the tears of mirth from her eyes. "And useful to have around, I hasten to add."

"Any further ideas on where and when we ought to launch *And Now?*" Abigail queried, casting her reproving glance at the noise her husband was making as he sucked the 'digestive' after dipping it in his tea, eyes closed and a look of sheer ecstasy resting in his face, telling the world at large that this was why digestives had been invented.

"Perhaps a similar place and time where we did our first signing?" Poppy returned with reminiscences dancing in her mind. "Blueberry's Bookshop in the North Riding, I believe, if it's still open."

"That it *is,* and they have staked their claim," Hal responded once his excitement had been assuaged, and his tea and biscuit had disappeared altogether.

"Staked their claim?" Poppy queried, with no idea what he was on about. "What does that mean?"

"The manager has ordered at least six hundred copies of *And Now?* if you can arrange a signing within the first week of its being released," Hal explained with an almost excited grin.

"Abigail?" Poppy said as she turned to her good friend. "Is that possible?"

"Jenny Wilton tells me that the book will be here in three weeks, give or take," Abigail offered.

"And what does that mean?" Hal asked sharply. "Don't we need to be much more certain? I mean…"

"It's not her," Abigail rejoined. "We are at the behest of the printer. It all depends upon the amount of printing work they have. We'll just have to wait for whatever they dictate."

A gentle rattling of the front door to Poppy's cottage drew their attention.

"Jenny?" Poppy gasped as she opened the door. "This an unexpected pleasure. Tea and crumpets?"

"I am the bearer of good news," Jenny said over tea. "*And Now?* will be with you, here the day after tomorrow."

"But I thought…?" Poppy reacted with shock, looking around at Abigail.

"Your full order of six hundred copies will be delivered a day later to Blueberry's Bookshop," Jenny replied quietly controlled. "So, now you will be able to arrange your first launch. It might be a good idea to order some copies of *Faithfully Yours*, too. There will no doubt be folks that haven't read that one and will need it before they can read the new one."

Once Abigail and family had departed for well-earned peace and quiet at home, a glorious silence crept into every corner of the cottage. Poppy loved their family including new baby Georgie, but she had always loved the solace and stillness that her life alone had dealt her, giving her time to think and plan and read. Now she had decided to set her new story into a new different genre and time, an enjoyably welcome body of research concerning some of her favourite authors from the mid-eighteenth and early nineteenth centuries was about to surround and immerse her. Jane Austen, Charles Dickens, Mary Ann Evans, Louisa May Alcott, Charlotte Brontë were all held in high esteem by Poppy.

She wasn't too sure about the modern machinery that had been installed into her Yorkshire igloo; the black, noisy, intrusive telephone just wasn't her thing. But still, she felt it might be silenced or removed if it intruded too much.

Sitting once more in her easy chair close by the wood burning fire, her mind inadvertently floated towards thoughts of George. How he had changed from a thoughtless, boorish and selfish oaf to a handsome, sophisticated and attractively desirable young man had her gasping mentally. Those difficult days in his presence before Poppy left for Southern France had vanished into another world. She looked forward to spending time with him and his remaining family throughout the days ahead.

A light knock at the front door awoke her from a shallow sleep that had crept upon her surreptitiously. Wary about opening the door to what could be an unknown stranger, she engaged the sturdy safety chain before answering the now urgent caller.

"Father! For goodness' sake come in!" she urged as she threw wide the door to him and his wife.

"Bad news, I'm afraid," he imparted sadly.

CHAPTER 30

The day after the wanderers returned from their sojourn on the French Riviera, George couldn't get Poppy out of his mind, almost bouncing backwards and forwards between the many episodes in their past relationships. After all this, he was left with one result … would he wish to rekindle a relationship of sorts? He had no answer to that one. So close so many times! He had no idea how another attempt might fare. Should he even contemplate the possibility?

"I have a slight inkling I know what is chasing about around your mind at the moment, Old Chap," Ross ventured as he caught up with his friend in their café. "I feel it has nothing to do with Southern France or the new flock of Blackface sheep you have before you."

"Perceptive, eh, Ross?" George responded eagerly.

"She was – is – very surprised yet pleased by how different you seem to be over the last time you saw each other," Ross returned with a grin. "She was right, of course. The last time you saw each other, *you* were a mess."

"Thanks for that, Friend!" George came back a self-deprecatory grin decorating his face. "She had a lot to put up with, I'm afraid to say, and it took me a significant amount of time and self-admonishment to see and change. All encouraged by my illness."

"Could have gone the other way completely, my friend," Ross agreed. "Then you might not have had a second chance."

"Second chance?" George asked. "Not sure about that. Time has moved along significantly since we were an item, so don't hold your breath."

"It seems to me that you still bear … feelings for her?" Ross rejoined reasonably sure of his opinion. "If that is the case, don't put your feelings on the back burner again. It's just that you need to be more forthcoming, but in a much more leisurely way. Softlee softlee catchee monkey."

"Not heard that saying before," George replied. "Did you make it up?"

"Lord Baden Powell, the scouts chap, in the mid-1890s, quoted a saying current in India where he spent some time," Ross explained. "Take things steadily and you'll achieve your goals."

"I bow to your clever words, My Lord Ross!" George said with a grin and a deep bow.

They both laughed at Ross's clever words that he had read … somewhere, but George took sensible note of what he was saying. Would he ever be able to win back his one-time true love? He doubted that but didn't dismiss the notion.

"Trouble, Father?" Poppy asked him as they sat by the fire, concern etched on her face. "Please tell me!"

"You know Sally was expecting our third child?" he suggested carefully.

"I had a hint," she said playfully.

"Well, she was delivered … stillborn," Sally butted in, tears streaming down her cheeks.

"Fortunately, we demanded the child's body so we could provide a proper burial for her," Tommy reacted. "She was beautiful … but not alive."

Sally's shoulders were moving noiselessly by this time with her husband's arms holding her heaving body close to his.

"We wanted her near us so we could celebrate her arrival and not allow her to be lumped into a mass grave where she wouldn't be recognised or acknowledged," Sally went on after she had begun to settle. "And we will be committing her frail little body into God's keeping for the time being."

"May I be allowed to be there?" Poppy said, her sadness obvious to her father, following a similar experience with Abigail and Hal's twin son, James.

"This is why we came to you today," Tommy explained. "The interment is next week on Thursday. Only a select few will be present, and we are glad you would like to be there. She would have been your half-sister, and a full sister to our other two little ones."

"How are they taking it?" Poppy asked trying to change the subject slightly. She was now beginning to feel the weight on her shoulders doubling in size, as she had been closely associated with each family in these difficult times. Not being a parent herself, she had little idea on the depth of feelings present when losing an infant.

"Surprisingly well, even though they don't know all the details," Tommy replied. "Although it means a lot to us, we don't want to make too much of an issue because Annie's old enough to understand what feelings and emotions are and can do to a person if not handled wisely."

"I understand perfectly," Poppy responded carefully. "This is the third time I have experienced emotions that make me feel like I am riding a rollercoaster. Firstly, my sister-in-law, whose baby died as he emerged from the womb, then my dear friend's twin son was also stillborn, and now you my dear Sally and my father. Somehow, we don't know if it might happen to us, healthy though we might be.

"Have you named your little daughter," Poppy went on after a few moments of painful silence. "And have you arranged her interment in a plot of land close to your local church?"

"But—?" Sally butted in, incapable of understanding the point of all this rigmarole.

"It is very important for each spirit to be named, I feel," Poppy insisted. "Then at least we can visit their place of rest bearing their name."

"Never thought about it in those terms before," Tommy returned, having given his wife a look and a slight nod.

"We had thought of calling her Annabel," Sally offered, "but because she didn't enter this world as a living being we—"

"Didn't see the point?" Poppy interjected quietly but calmly.

"Now I understand," Tommy added, turning to face his wife. "Perhaps we should rethink?"

⁓

"Have you thought about what you might do with your almost limitless time without even a pastime?" Ross Senior posed the difficult question to his soon-to-be son-in-law.

"I had a very successful taxi driving business in and around Richmond in Yorkshire's North Riding," Toby responded slowly after a moment's consideration. "But nothing else urges me to pursue its course."

"Will your savings sustain you for the foreseeable future?" Ross asked pointedly. "Bearing in mind that you will have a wife, and eventually, children to support and look after?”

“*That* I do not know,” Toby replied. “Hence my thoughts on seeing if I can afford to purchase a vehicle to use as a taxi.”

“I have something I want to show you,” Ross revealed as he made for his apartment outside door, beckoning Toby to follow.

Once they had reached the ground floor outside, Toby looked around, puzzled to try to see why he had been brought downstairs. And then he saw it! Why was Ross standing by a Lanchester Landaulette with something of a self-satisfied smile growing?

“Is this anything like the motor you had in England?” Ross asked as he looked the lad in the face.

“Exactly the same, except for one detail,” Toby responded quietly.

“Which is?” Ross asked, knowing full well what that detail was.

“Steering wheel on the wrong side!” Toby grinned. “Can I assume this motor is for me to buy? I would love to have it because it’s the foreign version of the one I had, except for the steering wheel. How much will it cost me, even though I have no idea whether I will be able to afford it.”

“Well,” Ross said, stroking his chin in what seemed to be a thoughtful way, “it will cost you a princely ... nothing. This will be my wedding present for you and Sarah.”

C H A P T E R 3 1

How comfortable was Poppy's cottage writing room now that she was able to sit at her desk in her cushioned swivel chair so she could just sit and … think!

To think that her second novel as a follow on to *Faithfully Yours* would be released within the following weeks at the shop where her love affair with her reading public had started! Whenever she relaxed in this room, thoughts of those dear friends she had lost almost always drifted into her mind to remind her why her life often felt empty.

She still missed desperately the friendship she had shared with Florence from being eight in 1877, during that wonderful Christmas at Boulders Wood. Alice's had been a surprise wedding when Poppy and Florence were on their European Grand Tour with Abigail and Cousin Hal, which lasted hardly any time at all. Still, she had been part of their time spent at the seaside when, as twelve-year-olds, the five true friends enjoyed a week's holiday on Yorkshire's east coast with Grandpa Ross and Nanny Nell.

Her close friend George Garside had promised that they perhaps might consider marriage, but he didn't have the patience to allow Poppy to achieve some of her life-time ambitions before agreeing to make that life-long commitment.

Although she felt deeply about him, she couldn't give up her freedom at that time to undertake her writing ambitions that were close to fruition. Confusion still reigned significantly in her mind, particularly when she saw him again a few days before, for the first time in an age. How did she feel about him now that he seemed to have improved in many personal ways? Would that perhaps he might have waited that couple of years or so before asking her that vital question!

A slight rattle of the door knocker caught her attention, bringing into sharp focus the time of day and the problems she had encountered in this cottage in years gone by. Gingerly she engaged the door's security chain, allowing her to open the door slightly.

"George?" she gasped quietly, seeing his face in the crepuscular light through the crack in the door. "Is it you?"

"Indeed, it is, Poppy," his familiar voice corroborated her thoughts as she opened the door to let him in.

"I haven't been able to get you out of my mind since I saw you a few days ago," he said quietly as they sat together on the sitting room's comfortable settee as they had done many years before. Those were the days when she felt excited about the future they had planned to spend together, when they were so madly in love, when nothing was going to stop their marriage.

This was the room, the settee where he had promised to spend the rest of his life with her as he held her tightly to him. This was the time she had agreed to marry him, at which he had sighed deeply "At last!"

Gently he took her hand in his, and, sliding his arm around her shoulders, he drew her unresisting body to him.

Turning her face to his she looked deeply into his eyes to

see if the look with which she had been captivated the last time had returned.

Did it matter? They would only find out by following their feelings from that particular moment.

Their lips met gently, passionately, telling them at that precise moment that they had found at last the love they had both been longing for.

And now…

Frank English
Author

Born in 1946 in the West Riding of Yorkshire's coal fields around Wakefield, he attended grammar school, where he enjoyed sport rather more than academic work. After three years at teacher training college in Leeds, he became a teacher in 1967. He spent a lot of time during his teaching career entertaining children of all ages, a large part of which was through telling stories, and encouraging them to escape into a world of imagination and wonder. Some of his most disturbed youngsters he found to be very talented poets, for example. He has always had a wicked sense of humour, which has blossomed only during the time he has spent with his wife, Denise. This sense of humour also allowed many youngsters to survive often difficult and brutalising home environments.

In 2006, he retired after forty years working in schools with young people who had significantly disrupted lives because of behaviour disorders and poor social adjustment, generally brought about through circumstances beyond their control. At the same time as moving from leafy lane suburban middle-class school teaching in Leeds to residential schooling for emotional and behavioural disturbance in the early 1990s, changed family circumstance provided the spur to achieve ambitions. Supported by his wife, Denise, he achieved a Master's degree in his mid-forties and a PhD at the age of fifty-six, because he had always wanted to do so.

Now enjoying glorious retirement, he spends as much time as life will allow writing, reading and travelling.

Other books for adults he has written:

Jack the Lad	Published 2016
Jack	Published 2016
Hit the Road Jack	Published 2017
Welcome Back Jack	Published 2017
All Right Jack?	Published 2019
Carry On Jack	Published 2020
Where to Now, Jack?	Published 2022
Hidden Secrets	Published 2021
Secrets Revealed	Published 2022
No More Secrets	Published 2023

Children's books he has written to date:

Magic Parcel: The Awakening	Published June 2010
Magic Parcel: The Gathering Storm	Published March 2011
Magic Parcel: A New Dawn	Published August 2012
18 Mulberry Road	Published September 2011
25 Primrose Walk	Published January 2013
Autumn Adventures	Published September 2013
Winter Tales	Published September 2014
Towards Spring	Published September 2016
Juniper's Tale	Published August 2018
Honey	Published January 2019
The Story of Lemuel Pecker	Published April 2019
Josephine's Journey	Published June 2019
Holly's Prize	Published April 2020
Garnett's Grand Getaway	Published May 2020
Sara's Astonishing Story	Published June 2020
The Boys in Black	Published August 2020
The Magic Whistle and the Tiny Bag of Wishes	Published October 2020
Half Moon Farm	Published March 2021
The Spirit Tree	Published February 2022
Mabel's Miraculous Manner	Published September 2022
Amalie's Amazing Adventures	Published September 2023
Believe	Published July 2024
The Adventures of the Lofthouse Family	Published September 2024

www.ingramcontent.com/pod-product-compliance
Lightning Source LLC
Chambersburg PA
CBHW020656120726
47906CB00001B/299